Hard to Be Good

Hard to Be Good

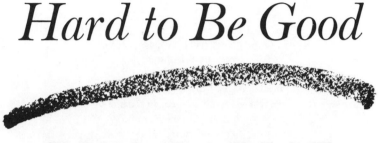

BILL BARICH

Farrar, Straus and Giroux

NEW YORK

Copyright © 1982, 1983, 1984, 1986,
1987 by Bill Barich
All rights reserved
Printed in the United States of America
Published simultaneously in Canada by
Collins Publishers, Toronto
First printing, 1987
Designed by Cynthia Krupat
Library of Congress Cataloging-in-Publication Data
Barich, Bill.
Hard to be good.
I. Title.
PS3552.A6163H37   1987   813'.54   87–19654

Grateful acknowledgment is made to The New Yorker,
where all these stories, except "Giorgio's Mother,"
first appeared, in slightly different form.
The title story was reprinted in The Best American
Short Stories, 1983, edited by Anne Tyler.

The author wishes to express his gratitude to the
John Simon Guggenheim Foundation for its generous
support during the writing of this book.

CONTENTS

HARD TO BE GOOD

S H A N E got arrested just before his sixteenth birthday. It was a dumb bust, out on a suburban street corner in Anaheim, California, on a warm spring night. A couple of cops were cruising through the haze and saw some kids passing around a joint, and they pulled over and did some unwarranted pushing and shoving, which resulted in a minor-league riot. Shane did not hit either of the cops, although they testified to the contrary in court, but he did break the antenna off their patrol car, so the judge was not entirely wrong to give him a suspended sentence and six months' probation. The whole affair was no big deal to Shane, since he didn't feel guilty about what he'd done—the cops had been *asking* for trouble—but it bothered his grandparents, with whom he'd been living for some time.

His grandfather, Charlie Harris, drove him home after the court appearance. Harris was a retired phone-company executive, stocky and white-haired, who had great respect for the institutions of the world. "I hope you know how lucky you are to get off easy," he said. "The judge could have thrown the book at you."

Shane was slumped in his seat, studying his fingernails. "It was a farce."

"You take that kind of attitude and you'll wind up in the penitentiary."

"I'm not going to wind up in any penitentiary. Anyhow, the cops didn't tell the truth."

"Then they must have had a reason," Harris said.

After this, Harris made several secretive phone calls to his daughter Susan, who was Shane's mother. She lived in the redwood country north of San Francisco with her third husband, Roy Bentley. Bentley was some kind of wealthy manufacturer. Shane heard only bits of the conversations, but he was still able to guess what they were about. His grandparents were fed up with him. They'd been on his case ever since his school grades had started to drop, and it did no good anymore for him to explain that his math teacher failed everybody who wasn't a jock, or that his chemistry teacher was notoriously unfair—to the Harrises, teachers were in the same unimpeachable category as judges, cops, and ministers.

So Shane was not surprised when his grandfather broke the bad news. This happened one night when they were watching the stock-car races out in Riverside. They both loved speed and machinery. After the next-to-last race, Harris put his arm around Shane and told him that Susan wanted him to spend a couple of months with her during the summer. He used a casual tone of voice, but Shane understood that something irreversible had been set in motion.

"It's because of the bust, isn't it?" he asked. "I said it wasn't my fault."

"Nobody's blaming you. Your mother just wants to see you. Things are going well for her now."

"You really think Susan wants to see me?"

"Of course I do," said Harris, giving Shane a squeeze. "Listen, this Bentley guy's loaded. He owns a whole ranch. Your mom says you can have a separate cabin all to yourself. You'll have a wonderful visit."

"Not when all my friends are here," Shane said. "What's there to do in Mendocino?"

"Same stuff you do here. Don't be a baby, Shane. Where's your spirit of adventure?"

"It dissolved."

Harris moved his arm. "If you're going to take that attitude," he said, "we won't discuss it any further."

"It's always *my* attitude, isn't it? Never anybody else's."

"Shane," said Harris, as calmly as he could, "you just simmer down. You're not always going to get your own way in life. That's the simple truth of the matter." He paused for a moment. "The important thing for you to remember is that we love you."

"Oh sure," said Shane. "Sure you do."

Right after school let out in June, Shane got a check in the mail from his mother. She sent enough for him to buy a first-class plane ticket, but he bought a regular ticket instead and spent the difference on some Quaaludes and a bunch of new tapes for his cassette player. The drive to the airport seemed endless. At the last minute, his grandmother had decided to come along, too, so he was forced to sit in the back seat, like a little kid. The space was too small for his body; he thought he might explode through the metal and glass, the way the Incredible Hulk exploded through clothes. He watched the passing landscape, with its giant neon figures, its many exaggerated hamburgers and hot dogs. It appeared to him now as a register of all the experiences he would be denied. He would have a summer without surf and beer, without friends, and possibly without sunshine.

The scene at the airport was as difficult as he feared it might be. His grandmother started sniffling, and then his grandfather went through a big hugging routine, and then Shane himself had to repress a terrible urge to cry. He was glad when the car pulled away, taking two white heads with it. In the coffee shop, he drank a Coke and swallowed a couple of 'ludes to calm his nerves. As the pills took hold, he began to be impressed by the interior of the terminal. It seemed very slick and shiny, hard-surfaced, with light bouncing around everywhere. The heels of people's shoes caused a lot of noise.

Susan had enclosed a snapshot with her check, and Shane removed it from his wallet to study it again. It showed his mother and Roy Bentley posed on the deck of their house. Bentley was skinny, sparsely bearded, with rotten teeth. He looked more like a dope dealer than a manufacturer. Shane figured that he probably farmed marijuana in Mendocino, where sinsemilla grew with such astounding energy that it made millionaires out of extremely improbable types. He hoped that Bentley would at least be easy to get along with; in the past, he'd suffered at the hands of Susan's men. She tended to fall for losers. Shane's father had deserted her when Shane was ten months old, vanishing into Canada to avoid both his new family and the demands of his draft board. Her second husband, a frustrated drummer for a rock band, had a violent temper. He'd punched Susan, and he'd punched Shane. Their flat in the Haight-Ashbury came to resemble a combat zone. It was the drummer's random attacks that had prompted Susan to send Shane to stay with her parents. He was supposed to be there for only a few months, but the arrangement continued for more than three years. Shane still hated the drummer. He had fantasies about meeting him someday and smashing his fingers one by one with a ball-peen hammer.

When Shane's flight was announced, he drifted down a polished corridor and gave his boarding pass to a stewardess whom he was sure he'd seen in an advertisement for shampoo. He had requested a seat over a wing, so he could watch the pilot work the flaps, and he had to slip by another young man to reach it. The young man smiled a sort of monkey smile at him. He was slightly older than Shane, maybe seventeen or eighteen, and dressed in a cheap department-store suit of Glen plaid.

Once the plane had taken off, Shane finagled a miniature bourbon from the shampoo lady and drank it in a gulp. The alcohol shot to his head. He felt exhilarated and drowsy, all at the same time. He glanced over at the young man next to him, who gave off a powerful aura of cleanliness, as though he'd been scoured with buckets and brushes, and said, without thinking much about it, "Hey, I'm really ripped."

The young man smiled his pleasant monkey smile. "It's okay," he said reassuringly. "Jesus loves you anyhow."

Shane thought the young man had missed the point.

"I'm not talking bourbon," he whispered. "I'm talking drugs."

"I guess I must have done every drug there is," the young man said. He tugged on his right ear, which, like his left, was big. "I can understand the attraction."

The young man turned out to be Darren Grady. His parents were citrus growers. He was traveling to a seminary outside San Francisco.

"You're going to be a priest?" Shane asked.

Grady shook his head. "It's more in the nature of a brotherhood. Maybe you've seen those ads in magazines asking for new brothers?" Shane had not seen the ads. "I never noticed them, either," Grady went on, chewing a handful of peanuts, "until I got the call. You want to know how I got it? I was tripping on acid at Zuma Beach, and I saw this ball of fire over the ocean. Then I heard the ball speak. 'Judgment is near,' it said. I'm not kidding you. This really happened. At first, I thought I was hallucinating, but it wouldn't go away, even after I came down."

"So what'd you do?"

"Went and saw a doctor at the free clinic. He told me to lay off the dope. So I did. But I couldn't get rid of the ball."

"That's what made you want to be a priest?"

Grady frowned. "I can never tell it right," he said, picking through the peanut dust at the bottom of his little blue-and-silver bag.

Shane was moved by Grady's story. He'd had similar baffling trips, during which his mind had disgorged images of grievous importance, but he'd never put a religious meaning to any of them. He felt foolish for bragging about taking pills. In order to set the record straight, he explained to Grady that he'd been exposed to drugs very early in life, because his mother had been a hippie; she'd named him after her favorite movie.

"It's not as bad as some names," Grady said. "I had a guy named Sunbeam in my class last year. Anyhow, you can go into court and get it changed."

Shane didn't want to see another judge, ever. "It doesn't bother me much now," he said, looking out at the sky. "When we lived in the Haight, Susan's husband, he was this drummer—he'd let me pass around joints during parties. Sometimes he'd let me have a hit. Susan knew, but I don't think she cared. I was so small, probably not much of it got into me. I don't know, though. I hate it when I see little kids smoking dope around school. You ought to be at least thirteen before you start."

"Maybe you should never start," Grady said.

"I wouldn't go that far. It helps to calm you."

Grady tapped his breastbone. "The calm should come from inside," he said.

It seemed to Shane that Grady was truly wise for his age, so he confided all his troubles. Grady listened patiently until he was done. "I don't want to downplay it, Shane," he said, "but I'm sure it'll be over soon. That's how it is with troubles. They float from one person to the next. It's bound to come clear for you real soon."

Shane's high had worn off by the time the plane landed. He and Grady took a bus into the city, and at the Greyhound station, off Market Street, they exchanged addresses and phone numbers. The light outside the station was intense, bathing bums and commuters. Shane was feeling relaxed, but he got anxious again when Grady left for the seminary. He was nervous about seeing Susan;

their last visit, down in Anaheim at Christmas, had been marked by stupid quarrels. He tried talking to a soldier who was also waiting around, but it didn't work. The soldier was chewing about four sticks of gum. Shane asked him to buy a bottle of apple wine, so they could split it, and when the soldier did Shane drank most of it, washing down two more pills in the process. He was semiconscious on the bus ride up the coast. The town of Mendocino, arranged on a cliff overlooking the Pacific, struck him as a misinterpretation of New England. "It's cute," he said, to nobody in particular.

From the lobby of an inn on the main drag, he phoned his mother, and then he fell asleep in a chair. Later, he heard somebody (he thought it was Susan) say, "Aw, Roy, he's ruined," so he said a few words in return and walked wobbly-legged to a station wagon. The next thing he knew, somebody was handing him a sandwich. He took it apart, laying the various components—cheese, tomatoes, alfalfa sprouts, two slices of bread—on the table. It occurred to him that he wasn't hungry. He said something to that effect, and somebody said something back—Bentley, the guy from the photo. He followed Bentley into a black night. Moisture from redwood branches dripped onto his head. Bentley unlocked the door of a cabin that smelled of pitch and camphor, and said something about extra blankets. Then Shane was alone. The whirlies hit him, and he stumbled to a small unstable bed. After he was under the covers, the whirlies subsided, and he was able to assess his surroundings. He thought they were pretty nice. The only thing that concerned him was that there seemed to be animals in the cabin—they didn't scratch or howl, but he was aware of them anyway, lurking just beyond his line of vision.

The animals were ducks, two of them, with bulbs inside glowing like hearts. Shane saw them when he woke in the morning. Gradually, he remembered where he was, along with the details of his arrival, and he felt disgusted and ashamed and yanked the covers over his head.

For some reason, he started thinking about Darren Grady. He was certain that Grady had never pulled such a dumb stunt. He wondered if Grady had made it to the seminary and if the other priests had shaved off his hair; he wondered, too, if Grady would recall their meeting or if all such mundane occurrences would automatically vanish from his mind, to be replaced by a steady image of God. Fifteen minutes or so passed in this fashion, helping to temper Shane's guilt and instill in him a new commitment to righteous behavior. He didn't pretend that he could ever be as wise and good as Grady, but he considered it within his power to improve. He got out of bed, examined the ducks more closely—they were lamps—and then, outside the cabin, he dumped his remaining pills on the ground and crushed them to dust. The act was like drawing breath.

Bentley's place was indeed like a ranch, fenced-in and isolated from any neighbors. There were a few outbuildings, including a chicken coop and a beat-up barn missing boards from its siding. Inside the barn, Shane found bird's nests, rusty tools, and a broken-down old Chrysler with fish fins. Parts from the Chrysler's carburetor were scattered on a shelf, leaking oil.

Shane expected to be jumped on as soon as he opened the door to the main house, but nobody seemed to be around. He had no memory of its interior, except as a series of difficult-to-negotiate planes and angles. In the kitchen, he poured himself a glass of orange juice and sat down to read the sports page of a day-old paper. He heard his mother call to him from upstairs. "Is that you, Shane?" she asked. "Come up here right now. I want to talk to you."

He poured more juice and went up. "Where are you, Susan?"

"In here. I'm taking a bath."

The bathroom door was ajar; steam escaped from within. Shane peeked and saw his mother in the tub, under a layer of froth and bubbles. Her hair was pinned up; it was thick, still mostly black, with a few gray strands. Shane thought she was immensely beautiful. He couldn't remember how old she was—maybe forty. The number was an ancient one, but he believed that it didn't really apply.

"Don't just stand there," she said. "It's drafty. Come in and shut the door." When he was inside, she said, "You look a little better today."

"Feel a little better," Shane said.

"How about a kiss for the old lady?"

He bent down, intending to kiss her on the cheek, but she lifted her arms from the water and hugged him. The sudden movement lifted her out of the soapsuds, so that her breasts were briefly visible. Shane had seen her naked before, countless times—in bathtubs and at nude beaches —but the quality of her flesh seemed different now, echoing as it did the flesh in the porn magazines that he hid in his room in Anaheim.

"Oh, Shane," she said, pushing him away, "you were such a mess last night. What happened to you?"

Shane put his hands in his pockets. "Me and this friend of mine, Grady, we bought a bottle of apple wine and drank it at the bus station." He was quiet for a second or two. "I'm sorry I did it."

"Well, you *should* be sorry. You gave us a real scare. When you behave like that, it makes me think you want me to feel guilty. I know I shouldn't have left you with Grandma and Grandpa for so long. You're my responsibility, and I've done a poor job of raising you."

Shane recognized this as therapist talk; Susan was always seeing one kind of counsellor or another. Left to her own devices, she would have sputtered and thrown something at him. Once, she'd almost beaned him with a ladle; another time, an entire needlepoint kit had whistled by his ear. "You can't *raise* me, Susan," he said. "I'm not spinach."

She laughed and looked directly at him. "No, you're not spinach. But you'd better be telling me the truth about last night. It better not be pills again."

"It's not pills."

"It better not be, because if you get caught fooling with them you could go to jail, you know. It's a violation of your probation. I don't understand how you got arrested in the first place. Who were those kids you were hanging around with?"

"There's nothing wrong with the kids," Shane said heatedly. "The cops started it. Anyway, Susan, since when are you so much against drugs? You used to smoke a joint every morning."

"I haven't smoked marijuana in years."

"Sure, Susan."

"Don't you dare talk to me like that, Shane," she said. "I'm your mother."

"I know."

"I'm not trying to be moralistic or anything. I just want you to keep out of trouble." She stood up in the tub; water dripped down her breasts, all down her body. "Give me that towel, will you, honey?"

He grabbed a towel from the rack and threw it at her, much too hard.

She pressed the towel against her chest. "*Now* what is it?"

"What do you *think* it is? Christ, Susan, don't you have any modesty?"

"I'm sorry," she said, suddenly embarrassed. "I forgot how old you are." She wrapped herself tightly in a terrycloth robe. "Go downstairs and I'll make us some breakfast."

The eggs she fried were brown and fertile, with brilliant orange yolks. She served them on red ceramic plates from Mexico. The colors made Shane's head swim, but he still ate with appetite. He was glad the confrontation with Susan was over. Their future together no longer seemed littered with obstacles. As she moved about the kitchen, banging pots and pans in that careless way she had, he felt a deep and abiding fondness for her, even though he knew that she had presented him with a complicated life by refusing to simplify her own. Charlie Harris called her a "nonconformist," and Shane supposed that he was right. He respected her independent streak, because he had a similar streak in him; they were joined in a bond forged of trial and error.

After Susan cleared the table, she gave him some towels to put in the cabin and told him that she was going into town. He wanted to go with her, but she wouldn't let him.

"I don't mind errands," he said. He wanted to see what Mendocino looked like when it wasn't scrambled. "I could help you carry bags and stuff."

"We'll go tomorrow," Susan said firmly. "I'll have more time then. Today I've got my yoga class and a doctor's appointment." She came up behind him and hugged him again. Her breasts pressed against his backbone. "I love you very, very much," she said. "Now go get yourself clean."

Shane went dutifully out of the house, but he was worried a little. The word "doctor" had an awful connotation, like "teacher" or "cop." He had a terrible feeling that Susan might be sick. So a new thing began to haunt him— he ought to have been a better son. He remembered how in March his grandmother had reminded him to mail a birthday card to Susan, and how he had gone to the pharmacy and bought himself a candy bar instead. What possible use would candy be when Susan was in her grave? "You're so selfish," he said to himself, kicking at a pine-cone. Every problem in the world, he saw, had its roots in some falling away from goodness.

That afternoon, around lunchtime, Shane was in the old barn, sitting behind the wheel of the Chrysler and staring at the bird-peopled rafters, when Bentley wandered in and interrupted his daydream, which had to do with driving at great speeds over the surface of the moon. In person, Bentley looked even more disreputable than he had in the photograph. He could have been a bowlegged prospector who'd spent the last thirty or forty years eating nothing but desert grit. His rotten teeth were like bits of sandstone hammered into his gums. "How's the boy?" he asked in a twangy, agreeable voice, leaning his elbows on the car door.

"The boy's fine," Shane said. "He's just fine."

"Well, I'm happy about that. I'd like to have the boy step from behind the steering wheel of the car so that I can have a chat with him."

Reluctantly, Shane got out of the car. His hands were balled into fists. Down in Anaheim, he'd decided that if Bentley was a puncher, he'd punch first.

"Take it easy," Bentley said. "I'm not going to hit you."

"Wouldn't put it past you to try," Shane muttered.

Bentley lifted an expensive lizard-skin cowboy boot and ground out the cigarette he'd been smoking against the sole. "I lost my taste for violence a long time ago," he said. "Course, if I needed to, I could still fold you up and put you in my pocket with the Marlboros."

"I'm warning you," Shane said, backing off.

"The trouble is, Shane," said Bentley, following him, "your mother and I got a good thing going, and I don't want some wise-ass punk from surfer land to come around and spoil it. You pull the kind of crap you pulled last night one more time, and I'll stick you into a Jiffy bag and mail you home to the old folks."

"You can't boss me around."

At this, Bentley chuckled a bit, revealing the stumps in his mouth. "Sure I can," he said. "So long as you're on my property, and living off my kindness, I am most assuredly your boss. And here's some more news, my friend—I'm putting you to work." When Shane protested, Bentley cut him short by jabbing him in the sternum. "I'm giving you two choices. Either you can work by yourself at the ranch, and do some painting and cleaning, or you can work with me at the factory."

"What's your business?"

"I'm a manufacturer."

"Yeah, but what do you manufacture?"

"What I manufacture," said Bentley, "is ducks."

They went to visit the factory in Bentley's station wagon, which smelled of stale tobacco and leather. "See that rise?" Bentley asked Shane, as they passed a sloping hillside off to the right. "If you were to walk to the top of it and then down into the gully, you'd come to another twenty-acre parcel I own."

"Do you have another house there?"

Bentley gave him a peculiar look. "No house, no nothing," he said. "It just sits. It's appreciating in value. We'll have a picnic there someday."

"My grandfather," said Shane, "he loves to barbecue."

"We don't barbecue," Bentley said. "What we do is eat that organic food that Susan cooks. The woman has a fear of meat." He turned on the radio; a country singer was singing about beer and divorce. "Listen here, boy," Bentley continued, "I want you to have a good time this summer. I'm not naïve about dope. I've done my share of it. But you have to learn yourself some moderation. Moderation is the key. You keep on abusing yourself the way you're going, you'll wind up in a pine box."

"My grandfather said I'd wind up in the penitentiary."

"That, too," Bentley said.

The factory was situated at the edge of town, in a concrete building that might once have been a machine shop. Inside, ten or twelve young longhairs, both men and women, formed an assembly line at long wooden tables. As Bentley had said, they were making ducks—or duck lamps—by gluing two pieces of heavy-duty celluloid around a metal stand that had a socket at the top for a bulb. Once the duck halves were glued together, they were secured with rubber bands and left to dry for a day or two. The excess glue was later wiped from the ducks with solvent, and they were put in cardboard boxes and cradled in excelsior. The wholesale price was twelve dollars a duck, but they were sold in trendy stores for as much as forty apiece. The materials came from Hong Kong.

Shane was shocked. His mind boggled at the notion that somebody could earn a fortune on celluloid ducks. The arithmetic didn't seem right. Forty dollars? Who'd pay forty dollars? A movie star? Were there enough duck-loving movie stars to provide Bentley with the capital to own a ranch and forty-odd acres? Apparently so. But Shane remained suspicious—the scam was too good to be true. He wished that Harris, who was always harping on the importance of hard work, could be there to watch Bentley as he lounged around the shop, smoking cigarettes and joking with his crew. Harris would go right through the roof; he'd say the whole shebang was un-American. Shane liked the atmosphere, though. Nobody treated the craft of duck making very seriously. Besides, a tall blond girl with ironed hair kept glancing at him from across the room; he fell into an immediate fantasy about her. He told Bentley he'd prefer to work at the factory instead of at the ranch.

"I'll start you in the morning," Bentley said. "You'll be a duck-packer. You'll pack so many damn ducks, you'll be quacking in your sleep."

They locked up after everybody had quit for the day.

On the ride home, Shane's thoughts drifted back to Susan, and he asked Bentley if anything was wrong with her.

"No way," Bentley said. "She's a fine, fine lady. Absolutely perfect."

"I mean, is she sick or anything?"

"Sick? No, she's not sick. She's just got some female trouble. When you get older, you'll learn that every woman has it sooner or later. They can't avoid it, and you can't help 'em with it. It's just something they have to go through on their own," Bentley said with a sigh. "We'll talk about it more when we get to the ranch."

But Shane didn't bring up the subject again (he was afraid of what he might hear), and Bentley volunteered no further information. Instead, they returned to the barn and played with the Chrysler until they were both covered with oil. They cleaned the points and plugs and reinstalled the carburetor. Bentley showed Shane how the engine had been modified to make it operate at maximum efficiency. "Let's fire up the sumbitch," he said, wiping his face on a polka-dotted bandanna. He let Shane sit in the driver's seat and try the ignition, but the engine wouldn't turn over. "Pump the pedal," he said. Shane pumped it and tried the ignition again. The engine roared. It sounded big in the barn, scattering robins and swallows into the dusk. Shane floored the pedal briefly and felt himself transported; energy ran through him as though he were a sieve.

After Shane had been at the factory for three weeks, he sent a postcard to his Anaheim pal Burt, the kid who'd actually hit a cop during the bust. He described his cabin, the redwoods, and the factory. "If you want to come up here," he wrote, "I can squeeze in another bed easy. And don't worry about me doing any you-know-what. I'm off that stuff for good."

Twice his grandparents called to see how he was getting along. He still felt estranged from them, and this was compounded when they told him they'd bought a camper and were going to Joshua Tree National Monument until mid-August unless Shane planned to come back before then.

"Me?" he asked, sounding wounded. "Since when do *I* have plans?"

For the next twenty-four hours, he was sullen and depressed, but he had to work at it, because he was having so much fun on the job. Every morning at eight, he and Bentley headed off together into a coastal fogbank that was always just beginning to disperse. They drank coffee from Styrofoam cups and told each other duck jokes while they watched the sky separate into a confetti mist under which the town of Mendocino stood exposed, back from wherever it went at night. Shane packed boxes with a ponytailed guy who was known as Eager on account of his last name, Beaver. Eager was anything but—he had a meticulous nature, and he took pains to be sure that each duck was nestled as comfortably as possible in its excelsior. He could have been packing eggs or glassware. "C'mon, Eager," Shane said to him one afternoon. "They're not alive, you know."

The tall blond girl was Emma King. She was nineteen, a college student. Shane followed her around like a dog. When the weather was hot, Emma came to the factory in white shorts and a red halter top, and Shane would monitor her every movement from his packing station, waiting for her to reach down for a tube of glue or bend low for the

X-Acto knife she kept dropping on the floor. She had a boyfriend she saw on weekends, but she told Shane that she'd go to the movies with him before he returned to Anaheim. "I'm in love with this heavy girl, she's *nineteen!!!*" he wrote on another postcard to Burt. "We go drinking together after work." This was almost true, or at least on the outer fringe of validity. One Friday, Eager *had* invited him to go to a tavern in the woods where anybody could get served, but he'd decided against it to avoid trouble. Later, he heard that Emma had been there, so in his mind they were linked.

He asked her for a photo, but she didn't have any, so he borrowed Susan's camera and snapped her in different poses, while she pretended to complain. The cutest shot was one of Emma kissing a duck on its beak. Shane taped it to the dashboard of the Chrysler. He thought of it as his car now. Bentley had promised it to him in lieu of wages if he could pass his driver's test. Already, he was practicing. He did Y-turns and parallel parking. Some evenings, he and Bentley took a ride to the ocean, steaming down dirt roads that were dotted with Scotch broom and beach poppies. Once, Bentley let him go by himself, without any adult supervision, and he handled the Chrysler with such authority and skill that he developed a stitch in his side from excitement. It was a mystery to him how things kept changing.

Another mystery was his mother. He'd never seen her so happy. He could not reconcile so much happiness, in fact, with scraggly, bowlegged, rotten-toothed Bentley. Here was a man who could walk around for days with egg in his beard and never even notice. The scent of nicotine was embedded in his clothes and maybe in his skin. Could it be that love had nothing to do with beauty? If Bentley could provoke love, then so could a stone or a twig. So could a garbage can.

But there was no denying Susan's contentment. She thrived on Bentley's generosity. She seemed to float around the house, gliding barefoot an inch or two above the floor, dressed in blouses and peasant skirts that showed off her bosomy fullness. She baked bread, hummed romantic tunes, and filled all her vases with flowers. She was constantly hugging her egg-stained lover, patting him on his flat little prospector's ass. The affection spilled over to Shane. Susan's arms were always grasping for him, making up for lost time. She drew him to her for purposes of both measurement and embrace. The very size of him seemed to thrill her—he'd grown from almost nothing! "Oh, Shane," she'd say in a husky voice, holding a hunk of his cheek between her thumb and index finger. "You're such a dear boy."

If Shane hadn't known better, he would have sworn that she was stoned all the time, but he'd never seen any dope in the house. As far as he could tell, the Bentleys had adopted a much more civilized vice. They drank wine— a bottle every evening, with Bentley leading the way. The wine burnished their faces. It made them talkative, sentimental, occasionally teary-eyed. After dinner, if the fog wasn't too thick, they'd put on sweaters and sit on the deck and speak in conspiratorial tones about the day's events, while bats sailed overhead, like punctuation. When there was nothing on TV, Shane sat with them, shivering no matter how many layers of clothing he wore.

"Thin blood," Bentley would say to him. "Goddam thin Southern California surfer's blood."

"My blood's fine."

"It's *thin*, Shane. It takes six months for blood to adapt to a new climate."

Blood was yet another mystery. Sometimes Shane thought that he understood Susan better than Bentley did, simply because they were related by blood instead of marriage. Although he and Susan had often lived apart, had quarreled and made mistakes, she was still his mother, and he was able, in a curious way, to anticipate her moods and know when something was bothering her. One night, as they sat outside, he saw that she was unusually quiet, removed from the conversation, and when Bentley went into the house he asked her if she'd got bad news at the doctor's office—she'd had another in her ongoing series of appointments that afternoon. The question made him tremble. Suppose she confessed something awful to him? Ignorance was a kind of protection. But she only smiled wistfully and patted his hand and said no, nothing very serious was wrong. It was just that the doctor had told her that she might need an operation—minor corrective surgery. She started to explain the problem to him in clinical terms, but it sounded indecent somehow to hear her describe her body as though it were an engine in need of repair, so he interrupted. "I know," he said, mimicking Bentley's sad resignation. "Female trouble." He put an arm around her, wanting to say more, but by then Bentley was back with full wineglasses and a word about the rising moon.

Shane's driving test was scheduled for a Thursday afternoon. Bentley gave him permission to come home early from work to practice. He backed the Chrysler into the barn several times without scratching it, and then he walked over to the house, hoping that Susan would make him a snack, but she'd gone to town for her yoga class. The phone rang while he was eating a boiled hot dog. Darren Grady was on the line, calling from Elk, a town south of Mendocino. Grady was upset, distressed, talking a mile a minute. He'd run away from the seminary and he was stranded, broke. Shane couldn't believe it. Where had Grady's wisdom gone? "Take it easy, Darren," he said. "Everything's going to be all right."

But Grady was blubbering. "I was trying to hitch to your place," he said, "but this highway patrol, he kicked me off the road. I cooled it in the bushes for a while and tried again, but here comes old highway patrol with his flasher on. I gave him the finger and split for town. I'm like a hunted criminal, Shane. You got to help me."

Shane glanced at the kitchen clock. He figured that he could get to Elk and back before he and Bentley were scheduled to meet the state examiner, so he told Grady to sit tight. The drive over there took about twenty minutes and gave him a severe case of paranoia. Every car that approached him seemed from a distance to be black and ominous and full of cops.

Grady was where he said he'd be, in front of a restaurant. He was sitting on the curb and eating a hamburger—some ketchup was on his chin—and drinking a can of beer. When he saw Shane, he waved wildly and let loose his monkey smile. Shane was surprised that Grady still had hair—there was no bald spot or anything. The only truly abused part of him was his Glen-plaid suit. All its department-store slickness had been rubbed away; there were holes in the knees of his trousers, as if he'd been on a long pilgrimage over concrete. Also, he'd lost his socks. The confidence he'd had on the plane was gone; now he was nothing but fidget. "I'll never forget you for this, Shane," he said, getting to his feet. "Is this yours?" he asked in wonderment, touching the Chrysler's fins. "It's a mean machine."

Shane eyed the half-demolished burger. "I thought you were broke," he said.

"I am, but I talked up the waitress in there"—Grady jerked his streaked face in the direction of the restaurant —"and traded her my Bible."

"She gave you beer for a Bible?"

"Just the hamburger. The beer I found."

This sounded fishy to Shane. "Where'd you find it?" he asked.

"Some guy left it on the seat of his car." Grady climbed into the Chrysler. For a moment, he seemed collected, drawn virtuously into himself, but then he fell apart and started bawling. "You're the only damn friend I've got," he said, blowing his nose in the hamburger wrapper.

Grady told Shane that he'd been on the road for three days. The first night, after he'd snuck out of the seminary, he hitched to San Francisco and slept in the Greyhound station, thinking he would catch a bus to Anaheim in the morning, but when he woke he realized that he'd have to confront his parents with the sorry evidence of his failure, so, instead of phoning them, he walked all the way to Fisherman's Wharf and ate a breakfast of crab and shrimp, and then spent twenty-two bucks playing video games at an arcade. This left him with just one dollar to his name—his emergency dollar, which he kept folded in sixteenths and hidden in the secret compartment of his wallet. When he pulled it out, the slip of paper on which Shane had written Susan's address and phone number fell to the floor.

"You get it?" Grady asked, turning toward Shane, who was paying only a little attention, since he had to watch for cops. "It was a *sign!*"

"What about the ball?" Shane asked. His forehead was wrinkled in concentration.

"Ball? What ball?"

"The ball from Zuma Beach. Did it come back while you were with the priests?"

"It never did."

"Then why'd you leave?"

Grady shrugged. His fidgety fingers picked at his knees through the holes in his pants. "It's hard to be good," he said. From the pockets of his suit coat he took two fresh cans of beer and—before Shane could protest—popped the tops. Shane accepted a can and stuck it between his thighs. He hit a bump and got doused.

On the second day, Grady said, he'd reached the town of Healdsburg. He said it was the hottest place he'd ever been to—hotter than Hell, frankly. In the evening, when it got too dark to hitch anymore, he wandered to the town square, where there were palm trees and flowers and benches, and he took off his shoes and socks and dunked his feet in a fountain. The water felt soothing as it swirled between his toes, but a bunch of Mexicans who were hanging around the square kept watching him, and he thought they might knife him or otherwise do him harm. He knew this was a silly fear, but it was fear nonetheless, so he gathered himself together in a hurry, slipped his wet feet into his shoes, and walked briskly down a side street that led him to a vineyard, where he curled up on the warm ground and slept the night away under cover of grape leaves. A flaming sun woke him at dawn. He couldn't find his socks. Their absence seemed to hurt him more than anything else. "Everybody knows you're running away from something if you don't have socks on," he said, biting his lower lip. "Who's going to stop for a person with bare ankles?" With this, he finished his beer in a gulp and threw the empty can out the window. The can rattled over the macadam, bounced two or three times, and rolled past the nose of a highway-patrol car that was parked in the bushes, waiting for speeders.

"Aw, Grady," Shane said.

Grady swiveled around to look back. "That's the guy I gave the finger to," he said.

Shane felt as though his body had been stripped of a dimension and then spliced into a deadly, predictable horror movie. He tried to imagine that the cop hadn't seen the can—or, better, that the cop had decided to overlook it—but this didn't work, since the cop had left his hiding place and was approaching the Chrysler at a steady clip. Shane gave Grady the half-full beer he had between his thighs, and Grady dropped down in the seat and drank it off, then shoved the empty into the glove compartment. The cop came closer. Grady looked again, and, panicked, said, "He's going to bust us, Shane. I know by his face."

"You don't know for sure."

The cop's flasher went on.

Grady sank lower in the seat. "I'm holding, Shane," he said morosely.

Shane didn't want to take his eyes from the road. "You're *what?*"

"I'm holding some speed. I bought it at that arcade." He showed Shane four pills. "Should I throw them out the window?"

The pills got swallowed—Shane couldn't think of any other way to dispose of them. He and Grady ate two apiece, which lent a hallucinatory edge to subsequent events. The cop was wearing reflector sunglasses, for instance, so that Shane was able to watch himself react to the words that bubbled from between the cop's lips when the cop pulled them over. The cop spoke of littering, of underage drinking, of operating a motor vehicle without a license and without what he called a vehicular-registration slip. Eyeless, he led Shane and Grady to his car and locked them in the back seat behind a mesh screen. The pills really took hold on the ride to the police station, and Shane was possessed by a powerful sense of urgency and he couldn't stop talking. He believed that he had an important message to deliver about the nature of goodness, and he delivered it ceaselessly—to the cop, to the officer who booked him, to the ink of the fingerprint pad, and to the cold iron bars of his cell.

Roy Bentley bailed out the boys. He came to the station with his attorney, a fashionably dressed man whose hair was all gray curls. The attorney seemed to know everybody around, and after a brief back-room conversation he reported to Bentley that the charges, except for littering, had been dropped. Bentley paid a stiff fine, then put the boys in his wagon and drove them to the ranch. They were amazed to be let go so quickly. "You must be important, Mr. Bentley," Grady said.

"You two are just lucky I've got some clout," Bentley told them. "A successful businessman is not a nobody up here. I'm a Democrat and I belong to the Rotary. But don't think it's over yet. You still got Shane's mother to face."

Susan exploded. There was no therapist talk this time. When Shane came through the door, slinking like an animal, she yelled and threw a pot holder at him, and then, so as not to be discriminatory, she threw one at Grady, too. She grabbed Shane by the hair and held him in place while she lectured him. She said he was an ungrateful little bastard, spoiled, indifferent, snotty, rotten to the core. He refused to argue, but in the morning, when she was almost rational again, he explained to her exactly why he had done what he'd done, so that she would understand that he hadn't been frivolous or irresponsible. "It was circumstances, see?" he said, sitting forward in his chair and kneading his hands. "I couldn't just leave him in Elk, could I? How would you feel if you called some friend of yours for help and the friend said no?"

"What about Roy, Shane?" she asked. "You could have phoned him at the factory, and he would have gone for Darren."

"But it was an emergency, Susan."

"The only emergency was that you didn't think."

The next day she was more forgiving, taking into account his unblemished record, and also the fact that he had been (at least to some extent) a victim of fate. She also agreed that Grady could stay in the cabin for a few days, provided that he let his parents know where he was. This Grady did. "Hello, Dad?" he said to his father, while

Shane listened in. "It's me, Darren, your son. Remember about the seminary? Well, you were right. It didn't work out."

In the cabin, Shane and Grady lay on their beds in the dark and had long philosophical discussions. Grady said that when he got home he was going to forget about religion and enroll in a junior college to study biology, so he'd have a grasp of how the universe was put together. "Science today," he said, "it has the answer to all the mysteries." Shane confessed that he was dreading his senior year in high school; he would be an entirely different person when he returned to that bleak, airless building, yet nobody would acknowledge it. "The system hates what's real," he said.

On more than one occasion, they talked about how strange it is that sometimes when you do everything right, everything comes out wrong. Grady had examples. "I gave my sister this kitten for her birthday," he said, "and she was allergic to it." Or, "Once when I was small, I washed my mom's car to surprise her, but I used steel wool and scratched up the paint."

Shane had other questions. "If it was me stranded in Elk," he asked, "would you have come and got me?"

"You know it," Grady said, with emotion crowding his throat.

Both of them took a solemn vow never to touch dope again, ever, in any form, no matter how tempted they might be.

Grady ended up staying for better than two weeks. Several important things happened while he was around.

First, Shane passed his rescheduled driver's test and celebrated by pinstriping the Chrysler and painting flames on both its doors. Then he asked Emma King to go to the drive-in with him. They went to a kung-fu double feature on a Friday night. She sat so far away from him that it seemed a deliberate attempt to deny his existence. He thought that maybe older women expected men to be bold, so after a while he walked his fingers across the seat and brushed them against Emma's thigh. She sneezed. He withdrew. Later, on the steps of her house, much to his surprise, she kissed him full on the lips and told him he was sweet. He knew it was the only kiss he'd ever get from her, so, driving home, he made a mental inventory of the moment and its various tactile sensations.

Next, on a Saturday afternoon, he and Grady took the Chrysler to the main beach, but it was crowded with townies throwing Frisbees to their dogs, and Shane suggested that they go instead to this great isolated spot even he had never been to before—Bentley's twenty undeveloped acres. They had to slide under a barbed-wire fence that had NO TRESPASSING and PRIVATE PROPERTY signs plastered all over it. The trail down into the gully was steep and overgrown; the gully, in fact, was more like a canyon, with a stream trickling through it, and vegetation sprouting from the soil. The vegetation was so thick and matted that it was almost impossible for them to distinguish individual plants, but one of the plants they *could* distinguish was marijuana. A few stalky specimens were growing wild, like weeds. All Shane's suspicions were confirmed—Bentley *was* a grower.

"That's why he had the attorney," he whispered to Grady.

"Are you going to say anything?"

"Uh-uh. No way."

But Shane's conscience bothered him. In the eyes of the law, Bentley was a criminal. Did this put Susan in jeopardy, too? Would she be considered an accessory to the crime? So Shane spilled the beans to Bentley. He told him about the find and waited for Bentley to react.

"Well, you got me, all right," Bentley said sheepishly. "I did grow me a few crops of Colombian down there a while back, before I met your mother, but the whole experience rubbed me wrong. I had a couple of brushes with John Law, and they made me real nervous. That's why I took my profits and went into ducks. Ducks are as legal as it gets."

"What about the plants we saw?"

"Must be volunteers. That happens sometimes. Stuff grows from old seeds, leftover seeds. We'll go pull 'em up."

They pulled up all the marijuana plants in the gully, arranged them in a pyre, and burned them. "It's sad," said Bentley, leaning on a pitchfork and wiping his brow. "But it has to be."

Next, Susan went into the hospital for her operation. The surgery was performed in the afternoon, and Shane was allowed to visit that evening. He was scared. Susan was in a private room. She was still groggy from her anesthesia, and she had an I.V. tube in her arm. He thought she was asleep, but she called to him in a funny, childlike voice and asked him to sit in a chair by the bed. "I'm in the clouds," she said, rubbing his hand.

"But are you okay?"

"I'm fine," she said. "The doctor fixed everything. He says I can probably have a baby now."

"A *baby?*"

"You think I'm too old, don't you?"

"I don't know. How am I supposed to know about babies?"

"Lots of women have babies at my age," Susan said, rubbing and rubbing. "Roy and I want to try. Oh, Shane honey, I made things so tough on you, I want another chance. Don't I deserve another chance?"

"Sure," said Shane. "Of course you do."

But the potential baby confused him, and also depressed him a bit. In his mind, it was rotten-toothed, bearded, and smelling of tobacco. He wondered why Susan would want to introduce such a creature into the world. "I'm never going to understand anything," he complained to Grady that night. "Not anything."

"What's there to understand?" Grady asked.

"Maybe you are wise, Grady," said Shane.

Grady left at the end of the week. Shane dropped him at the Greyhound stop in Mendocino. They shook hands in a special way they'd devised, with plenty of interlocked fingers and thumbs.

"I never had a friend like you before," Grady said. "I'll never forget what you did for me."

"I'd do it again," said Shane. "Any time."

In late August there was an unseasonal thunderstorm. It rattled windowpanes and made chickens flap in their coops. When it was over, the morning sky was clear and absolutely free of fog. Shane got up early and changed the oil in the Chrysler. He packed the trunk with his belongings and put a pair of ducks for the Harrises on the back seat. Susan was not fully recovered from her surgery, so he had to say goodbye to her in her bedroom, where she was propped up against pillows. She asked him again if he didn't want to transfer to a school in Mendocino and stay on with them, but he told her that he missed his grandparents and his friends. "I might come back next summer," he said, kissing her on the cheek. "You'll probably have the baby by then." Bentley stuck fifty dollars in the pocket of his jeans. "You ain't such a bad apple, after all," said Bentley with a smile. Shane drove off quickly, without looking back. The highway was still slick and wet from the rain, and the scent of eucalyptus was in the air.

OCTOBER

THE GUEST who found Wilhelm Klemper in the bathtub at the Hotel Ghiberti was a woman. She screamed so loudly that Massimo, the night clerk, came running down the hall, from the lobby, carrying the heavy stick he had always hoped to use if an intruder appeared while he was on the job. Massimo was big and dark, with knitted brows and dreams of power. He glanced at the distraught woman, offered an apology, then burst through the bathroom door. In the tub he saw Klemper, the auto salesman from Munich, who was snoring peacefully, with his hands folded over his belly and his parted lips giving off a vapor of stale wine. "Herr Klemper," said Massimo, tapping him on the shoulder. Klemper kept right on snoring. Massimo, upset, shook him harder, and discovered that in fact Klemper was wedged in extremely tightly—stuck, so to speak. The *padrone*, Arturo Feraci, would have to be called.

Feraci was Massimo's father. He slept in a room at the rear of the hotel, as far away from the desk as possible. Unlike his son, he was built on a miniature scale, so that his features had an artistic perfection, as though they'd been planned in advance instead of molded by the usual give-and-take of reproduction; and he needed at least nine hours of sleep every night to restore his delicate energies. Massimo entered the bedroom deferentially, pausing for a moment to stare at the photograph of his mother that occupied a position of honor on the bureau. She was in Heaven, singing with the angels—that's what Massimo had been told by Feraci when he was a little boy, and he still believed it in a halfhearted way. Heaven was becoming somewhat less real to him as he grew older, even though he kept bumping into manifestations of it all over the city of Florence, in churches, chapels, monasteries, and museums. It was gold, brilliant, full of promise, but Massimo, at eighteen, was more interested in owning a Vespa. He approached the bed, where his father's humped form was hidden beneath a quilt, and, feeling guilty, reached out to tap it, much as he'd reached out toward the man in the bathtub.

"Eh?" asked Feraci.

"Herr Klemper," Massimo said in a hushed voice.

The name had a profound effect on Feraci. He threw back the covers, sat up in bed, and whispered something unintelligible. His fine gray hair, ordinarily arranged so neatly that not a speck of baldness showed, rose in wisps toward the ceiling.

"Drunk?" he asked.

"Of course," said Massimo.

"Is he alone?"

Massimo nodded, and Feraci sighed in relief. The last time Klemper had turned up drunk, he'd brought along a prostitute, and there had been a terrible scene in the lobby, during which Klemper had wept and issued his usual denials. For ten years now, he had been arriving promptly at the Ghiberti every October, dragging the same two leather suitcases and emanating the same good cheer. He had the salesman's knack for easy friendship. There were kind words for the *padrone*, hugs for the chambermaids, a new joke for Massimo. Was it possible to dislike him? Feraci doubted it. Klemper, with his abrupt and innocent eyes, seemed such a happy, carefree person that he was regarded affectionately by the entire hotel staff. And yet toward the end of his annual two-week vacation something always went wrong. Klemper stopped studying the Renaissance art he claimed to love and instead began to drink and carouse. He came in at odd hours, paying no mind to the curfew and waking the other guests. He violated house rules by bringing cheese and salami into his room and leaving them in drawers. He broke things—water glasses, pictures, once a mirror. Klemper was always deeply sorry when he returned to his senses, and Feraci, being a gentleman of the old school, had in the past always forgiven him for his transgressions. But no more. After the episode with the prostitute, Klemper had vowed never to misbehave again, and now that vow was worthless.

"Finito," Feraci said to Massimo as he slipped into a red robe that made him look like a cardinal. "Klemper must go."

Together, they marched down the corridor toward the bathroom where Klemper was trapped. It was dawn. Through the windows of the hotel, they could see the sun throwing light across the bright tile roofs. Somewhere a rooster crowed. The woman who'd screamed was waiting near the bathroom, along with her husband and another guest. They had the half-startled, half-curious expressions of people who gather at roadside accidents. Feraci smiled and greeted each of them by name, exuding such casual gallantry that his electrified hair went unnoticed. *"Permesso,"* he said softly, stepping past the guests to peer in at the problem. Klemper had not moved. His lips continued to give off vapors. Feraci was tempted to turn on the shower, but he thought that such blatant cruelty (however much it was deserved) might compromise the moral strength that was building in him. So instead he summoned Massimo. He assigned his son to Klemper's feet, then knelt by the tub and worked his own hands into Klemper's armpits. It took a great deal of pulling and shoving to liberate Klemper, who did not even wake up until Massimo splashed a little water on his face. He was groggy, indifferent, limp as a rag doll. Feraci helped him to stand and then led him to his room, where he collapsed in a heap on the disheveled bed.

Once Klemper was covered with blankets, Massimo was anxious to leave—he was taking a course in economics at the university—so Feraci kissed him on both cheeks and sent him away. A maid was brewing coffee in the kitchen. The vibrant aroma sailed toward Feraci, reminding him that, in spite of Klemper, there was still much to be savored in life. He was a man who believed devoutly in orderliness. To his ear, trained on Verdi and Puccini, the world hummed like a chord when everything was in its proper place. Any break in his daily routine bothered him, perhaps more than it should have. This almost spiritual dedication to order had always been a part of his character, but it had become more pronounced in the years since his wife's death. He had not married until he was nearly thirty-five, preferring to sift cautiously through potential brides until he found the right one, so he had been particularly wounded by his misfortune. He learned that habit was a good weapon against loneliness, even against despair—it cut down the field of vision. At any rate, Feraci was mystified by Klemper's apparent need for chaos. What was it that made the poor salesman erupt?

After breakfast, he dressed in a neatly pressed suit, sat in his chair behind the desk in the lobby, and began to perform the many services that had made his hotel a favorite with tourists of every nationality. He phoned for taxis, booked tables at restaurants, changed dollars into lire and lire into francs. Nothing in his manner suggested that he was nervous about his forthcoming encounter with Klemper, but he was boiling inside. He hated conflict—it was brutish, primitive. Over and over again, he played out the inevitable scene in his mind, resolving this time to do what was necessary.

Klemper did not come out of his room until early afternoon. As ever, he looked scrubbed and healthy. He had fantastic recuperative powers. His skin was rosy and he smelled of good cologne. Some shiny cream glistened in the bristles of his close-cropped hair. He was whistling.

How can it be, Feraci wondered. The man is shameless.

There was an awful jangle when Klemper dropped his key on the marble desktop. "Today, I go to the Bargello and visit Michelangelo," he said, grinning broadly, so that the gap between his two front teeth was exposed.

"We must have a talk, Herr Klemper," said Feraci in a dramatic, overly rehearsed voice. He spoke in English; it was their only common language.

Klemper put an elbow on the desk and rested his chin

on his palm. He had a shaving nick near his left ear, produced, certainly, by shaking fingers.

"A talk?" he said. "But must you be so formal, Signore? After all, we are old friends."

"Of course," Feraci said. "You are a friend. That is why the talk is painful to me."

"Painful?"

"Herr Klemper, I will say it out to you—you behaved badly again last night."

"Me?" asked Klemper. "You must be mistaken."

Feraci shook his head. "There is no mistake. Again you drank too much, sir. Don't you have any memory?"

Klemper's lower lip trembled. All at once his face lost its healthy glow and went through several quick transmutations, which left it looking babyish and wan.

"You woke the other guests," Feraci said, proceeding boldly. "You fell asleep in the bathtub. A woman screamed. I cannot have it anymore, Herr Klemper. You broke your vow."

"The trattoria where I ate, it wasn't very clean," Klemper said. "The wine must have been poisoned."

Involuntarily Feraci scratched his knee. "I must ask you to leave, sir," he said.

"I am sorry," Klemper told him. Tears were forming in his eyes. "I don't know what came over me. I promise you, Signore, it will never happen again."

"This I have heard before," said Feraci, crossing his arms. "I can't have it, Herr Klemper. My reputation is at stake."

Klemper was weeping openly now. When he was able to pull himself together, he said, "The Ghiberti means very much to me."

"I know that," Feraci said. "But still I ask you to leave."

"I will go in the morning."

"No, Herr Klemper. You must go today."

"*Today!*" wailed Klemper. "Today I am visiting Michelangelo at the Bargello!"

"You can find another hotel in Florence. There are hundreds, sir."

"Not like this one," Klemper said bitterly. "How can you do this to an old friend? What have I done to merit this treatment?"

Feraci was prepared for the question. He ran through the entire catalogue of infractions, leaving out nothing, not even the prostitute.

Klemper was stung. Clearly, he had never realized how his errors in judgment had been compounded over the years. "You are right, Signore," he said. "I have behaved very badly."

"And I must ask you, Herr Klemper," said Feraci, pushing on, "never to come here again."

"Never again?"

"This is correct."

Klemper stared at the floor, shuffling his feet. He seemed resigned to his punishment. "I understand," he said.

The conversation left Feraci feeling pleased. It was not so much a personal victory as a victory for the forces of order. He had managed to wrestle reality into a posture of accommodation; the scene with Klemper had taken place just as he'd imagined it. But Feraci didn't gloat—there was tragedy, too, in what had happened. When Klemper returned to the lobby with his luggage, Feraci stepped from behind the desk to help him. He thought of several conciliatory things he might say, but he suppressed them, not without difficulty. He watched Klemper squeeze his bulky body into the elevator. Klemper's face, bloodless and sad, filled the frame of the elevator-door window. *"Arrivederci,"* Feraci said. Down the shaft went Klemper, disappearing.

The cold winds that blow through Florence every winter came early that year, and the tourists, as always, were swept away—off to Greece and Portugal, where sunshine takes precedence over art. By December, the Hotel Ghiberti was almost deserted. This was not depressing to Arturo Feraci. He'd never wanted to be rich. Besides, a bit of solitude was good for the soul. He used his free time to make repairs, to redecorate and plan for the future. At Christmas, he closed down for three weeks and decided to go skiing in the Dolomites. Massimo went with him. They stayed at a pine-paneled lodge where the food was excellent but the rooms lacked character. "I would never permit this," Feraci said, showing Massimo the dust beneath a bed. Feraci's skin got tanned on the slopes, his muscles felt unusually supple. Is that a man of sixty, he asked himself one morning as he stood before his mirror. On Christmas Eve, he gave Massimo a big check, on the condition that it be put toward the purchase of a car, not a Vespa. "Motorcycles are too dangerous," he told his son.

Perhaps the expansiveness of the vacation, with its seemingly imperishable images of snow and sky, contributed to the romantic spirit that captured Feraci in the spring. Had daffodils ever burst through the earth with such brilliant determination? The beaks of blackbirds looked far too orange. Then Feraci fell in love. It was not something he had expected ever to happen again. The woman,

Gloria Bailey, was divorced, an American from Detroit who was touring the art capitals of Europe with five other women. She was in her forties, and she had a personality that combined brashness and charm in equal measure. She couched her affection for Feraci in teasing terms. "With a build like that," she told him one afternoon, admiring his trim figure, "you ought to be on display somewhere." Feraci burned with embarrassment, but the next day he invited her to lunch. Immediately he regretted it. Had he taken leave of his senses? It was wrong to flirt with guests. The lunch was a grand success, though, with so much intimate talking back and forth that Feraci's jaw actually began to ache. He was confused, miserable, ecstatic, torn; in a daze, he sought the counsel of his son.

Massimo was outside, waxing the little, used Fiat he'd bought. He listened to his father's lament until he couldn't stand it anymore. "Stop worrying yourself, Papa," he said. "Just be happy."

So Feraci tried. He accepted happiness as it was presented to him. There were more lunches, a carriage ride through piazzas lined with potted flowers, and then an astounding night of champagne and black lace, during which he recalled many pleasurable things he'd all but forgotten. When the other tour-group ladies left for Rome, Gloria stayed behind, explaining that she had not yet exhausted the possibilities of the Renaissance. Really, though, she had nothing pressing to take care of at home —her children were grown, she had no steady job. Soon enough, her clothes were hanging in Feraci's closet. She insisted on helping with the business. Feraci was afraid she'd make a botch of it, but she was very professional, measuring up to the most rigorous standards. In June, still slightly confused, he proposed to her, and they were wed in a small private ceremony, much to Massimo's delight. For their honeymoon, they had a quick weekend at Viareggio, by the sea. Massimo drove them there, proceeding at breathtaking speed, for he could not touch any steering wheel without pretending that he was in a Grand Prix. Along the way, Feraci's straw beach hat blew out the window. He wanted to chase after it, but Massimo convinced him that it was irretrievably gone, tumbling through pine seedlings and brush toward the water.

October, the month for game. Feraci took Gloria on his annual pilgrimage into the Tuscan hills, and introduced her to an old farmer from whom he bought venison steaks and wild boar. In exchange, Gloria taught Feraci to be a tourist in his own city, leading him through cobbled streets that were finally beginning to be free of summer people. They went to the Duomo and the Baptistery, and then to the Uffizi, where they climbed the stairs together, hand in hand, and walked into the gallery and fell silent in the presence of so many famous paintings. Feraci was thrilled. How could such familiar things still retain their power? "I haven't been here for ages," he said, wandering off alone, down precise, sunlit corridors lined with busts and portraits in orderly formation. He remembered walking through the museum with Massimo, years ago, trying to answer the boy's innocent but complex questions about death by directing his attention to the flaming gold on the walls. He had relied on the angels; they had not let him down.

From the Uffizi they went to the church of Santa Croce. Feraci did his best to appreciate the church's façade, but he was getting tired. The leg muscles he'd built up in the Dolomites were not so strong anymore, and he was starting to suffer the minor foot pains that seemed always to accompany an overdose of art. There was nothing at Santa Croce that he wanted particularly to see. It was a cavernous place, musty and damp, filled with pulpits, altarpieces, statues, crucifixes, relics, and other religious items that the Franciscans had managed to collect over the centuries. Feraci, separated from Gloria again, proceeded along the nave with none of the furious energy that had possessed him elsewhere. For the most part, he craned his neck and stared at the ceiling in an attempt to figure out how the various structural elements had been laced together. Because the church was crowded, Feraci, in his shuffling, could have bumped into anyone; but the one he did bump into was Wilhelm Klemper.

Klemper was standing by himself in an area of the church into which heat seemed never to have penetrated. His feet rested on a marble slab that bore the featureless portrait of some departed bishop; his eyes were fixed on a sculpture of the Annunciation.

"*Scusi,*" said Feraci after he'd made contact.

"Oh!" said Klemper, jumping back. "Signore Feraci!"

Feraci squinted at the face in front of him. "Is it you, Klemper?"

"It's me," Klemper said.

They shook hands politely. Feraci noticed that Klemper's flesh was clammy.

"Have you been here long?" he asked.

"Hours."

"Well," said Feraci, at a loss for words.

Klemper smiled tentatively. He seemed equally ill at

ease. "It's nice to see you again," he said. Then he nodded at the sculpture. "I like that," he said. "It's the only thing in here I understand."

"But I thought you loved all our art."

"I do," said Klemper, shrugging, "even though it depresses me."

"Perhaps we can sit down for a minute," Feraci suggested. "A rest would be good."

They found an unoccupied pew and sat on it. Feraci was keenly aware of Klemper's body next to him, and also of the hundreds of candles flickering throughout the church. He was glad to be so tired. It made him feel less nervous about the meeting.

"Well," he said again. "I am surprised."

"Surprised?" asked Klemper. "But why? I always come to Florence in October."

"Of course," said Feraci, who had meant no offense. "And you are having your usual fine time?"

"Not too bad. I am staying at the Cellini. Do you know it? It's near the train station."

"I don't know it, but I think it has a good reputation?"

"Very good," Klemper said. "But it's noisy."

"And the food?"

"All right, if you like fennel."

Feraci began idly to crack his knuckles. When he had finished with his right hand, he went to work on the left.

"How is Massimo?" Klemper asked.

"Fine," said Feraci. "But he isn't around so much anymore, now that he has a car."

"A car? What type of car?"

"Fiat."

"I hope you didn't pay full price," Klemper said. "I could have given you a discount on a Volkswagen."

"The Fiat was also discounted," Feraci replied. He did not want to seem rude or ungrateful, so he offered a bit of personal information. "I got married, you know."

"I heard," said Klemper. He had shifted his position and now sat with his elbows on his knees, in a droopy attitude of despondency. "That American woman."

Feraci was taken aback. "But *how* did you hear?"

"I asked about you at the Cellini. You must forgive my curiosity. The old ties are difficult to break." Klemper sighed. The sigh went on for a considerable time, owing to the width and depth of his chest, and the magnitude of air it contained. "Tell me, Signore," he said, "were those things I did really so bad?"

"Yes," said Feraci emphatically. "They were bad."

Again Klemper sighed. "I suppose that's that, then. The other night, when the traffic kept me awake, I almost called you to ask for another chance. But I didn't think you'd give it to me."

"I wouldn't," Feraci agreed.

"That's what I thought."

But in fact Feraci was losing his resolve. It had never occurred to him that he would see Klemper again, especially in such a cold and pitiable condition. He was seized by a desire to make amends; the desire was counterbalanced by a sincere belief that Klemper would repeat, in one form or another, his past outrages.

"Did I mention that I've moved?" Klemper asked.

"You didn't mention," Feraci said. He was hoping to end the conversation and be on his way.

"The company transferred me to Düsseldorf. It happened right after I returned from Florence last year. I have a much smaller territory now. You remember my house in Munich?"

Feraci nodded. Klemper had showed him photos of an impressive Tudor structure surrounded by trees.

"I had to sell it at a loss," Klemper said. "The real-estate market, it's terrible." Suddenly he reached down and rolled up a leg of his trousers. "Feel my knee."

"I couldn't."

"Anyway, it's like jelly. You see how it floats around? Some days it hurts so bad I go through a whole bottle of aspirin. They say I need an operation."

This was all Feraci could tolerate. He rattled off a string of excuses for leaving, which included Gloria, Massimo, and his own aching feet.

Klemper, of course, was distressed. He fiddled anxiously with the knot of his tie. "It's a pity," he said. "We have so much in common, we could probably talk forever."

Feraci smiled, bowed a little, pressed Klemper's clammy flesh, and escaped. He and Gloria took a taxi to the hotel. His meeting with Klemper haunted him, though; it had an unresolved quality about it, and he couldn't put it out of his mind.

So it was that on the following morning Feraci phoned Klemper and invited him to spend what remained of his vacation at the Ghiberti. Klemper, overjoyed, arrived within the hour. "You'll never regret this," he said, hugging the *padrone* so tightly that he seemed to be trying to extract juice. Feraci gave him an isolated room off the lobby. The visit proceeded without incident, except for the afternoon when Klemper dropped a teacup and broke it. But everybody judged this to be an accident. Klemper's behavior was otherwise exemplary. He made the rounds of churches and museums, just as he always did, and returned from them in a sober, contemplative mood. Often, he sat in the lounge of the hotel, reading a thick art-history book and writing marginal notes. Gloria talked to him a few times and reported to Feraci that he was something of an expert on the Renaissance. Massimo, on the other hand, was easy prey for Klemper's jokes and funny stories; he thought Klemper should be on television. Feraci regarded all this with a jaded eye; to him, the pattern was familiar, and he kept expecting Klemper to lose control at any minute.

But the days continued to pass calmly, and soon Klemper was making plans to go home to Düsseldorf. He insisted that he be allowed to show his appreciation to the Feracis by taking them out to dinner on the night before his departure. No ordinary restaurant would do—Gloria must choose some special place. It was agreed that everybody should meet in the lobby at seven o'clock; meanwhile, Klemper was off for a last look at the glories of Florence.

The Feracis were in the lobby at seven, but Klemper was late. When he hadn't come by seven-thirty, Massimo decided to go outside and wait in the car; Gloria went into the kitchen to consult with the cook about tomorrow's menu. This left Feraci alone at the desk, thumbing through a newspaper. Around eight o'clock, Klemper burst through the door. There was no question that he'd been drinking. He had a half-empty bottle of brandy under his arm, and he lurched when he walked. Another guest, a haughty Frenchwoman who'd just finished using the lobby phone, made a sound of disapproval when Klemper knocked over a lamp. In response, Klemper smiled his gap-toothed smile and sang a bawdy version of the "Marseillaise."

Feraci watched the entire performance. It had a curious effect on him. He was not so much angry as comforted.

"My friend!" Klemper bellowed, stumbling toward him. "How glad I am to see you."

"You are a fool, Klemper," said Feraci. "I knew you couldn't change."

"Oh, I *could* change," said Klemper, wagging a finger in Feraci's face. "I just don't want to." He laughed loudly. "I have a present for you," he said, removing what appeared to be a piece of stone from his pocket.

Feraci picked up the stone and knew immediately by its smooth exterior that it was marble. Looking more closely, he saw that the marble had a distinct shape. "This is a toe."

Klemper laughed again and patted him on the back.

"Where did you get it?" Feraci asked, dropping the toe into a drawer so that none of the other guests would see it. "Have you stolen it from a museum? Did you commit some crime?"

From another pocket Klemper produced a hammer. "Tap, tap," he said. "Bye-bye, Michelangelo."

"You broke it from a statue? A Michelangelo?"

"Could be a Michelangel. Could also be a Donatello."

"I am calling the *polizia*," Feraci announced.

But he was interrupted by Gloria, who'd heard the ruckus all the way in the kitchen. To his surprise, she didn't care about Klemper's drunkenness; she was so hungry she was willing to overlook almost anything.

"So he's had a little too much, Arturo," she said, slipping into her coat. "So what? Let's get going."

"Impossible." Feraci was adamant. "An outrage has happened."

"Okay, we'll go without you."

The Fiat was at curbside, warmed up, with its radio blaring. Massimo, who was also hungry, gunned the engine. He drove with even more than his customary panache, urged on by Klemper, who giggled whenever the brakes squealed. Feraci, in the back seat, was agonized; the speed was a kind of punishment, and so was the feeling that he was being dragged somewhere against his will. "If you don't slow down, Massimo," he shouted, "you're going to kill someone!" That wasn't what happened, though. Instead, Massimo wheeled too close to a parked car while he was turning a corner and smashed in his right front fender.

The damage to the Fiat wasn't bad, but by the time Massimo had found the owner of the other car and talked to her, they were later than ever for their dinner reservation. Their table had been given away, and they had to wait nearly an hour for another one. That it was in a terrible location, back in an alcove hung with Chianti flasks and haunches of prosciutto, seemed only proper to Feraci; once established, chaos expanded at an alarming rate. He glared at Klemper, who was pouring wine; the wine rose to the lip of the glass and spilled over onto the tablecloth.

For a first course, they ordered *crostini*—slices of grilled bread topped with chopped liver—followed by pasta. When Gloria had finished eating, she pushed away her plate and lit a cigarette. Through the smoke she noticed a mural on the opposite wall. The mural was meant to simulate a Renaissance fresco, and it showed saints and cherubs wandering aimlessly about in an unidentifiable landscape. No Florentine would have commented on it, for such paintings were common even in dumpy trattorias, but Gloria was still enough of a tourist to be curious.

"Oh, look," she said, pointing.

Massimo glanced up from the napkin on which he was trying to calculate how he'd pay for the Fiat's repairs. "Heaven," he said absently, recalling his childhood lessons.

"Heaven?" asked Klemper, in a voice that was both ironic and challenging. "How can that be Heaven?"

"The angels," Massimo said, sounding intimidated. "The halos. All the gold."

Klemper seemed not to hear. He was staring intently at the mural. "That's no kind of Heaven," he said. "I've been studying it for years. So flat and plain, so perfect, with nothing human in it. Who'd want to go there? It's horrible, isn't it?"

"Still," said Feraci, wiping his mouth, "it's Heaven."

"Maybe for you."

"For everybody."

Klemper smirked; he drank his wine, refusing to say anything more. He fell asleep during the fruit-and-cheese course, dozing off so suddenly that he rocked back in his chair and toppled to the floor. Feraci and Massimo hauled him to the car, and then, with the assistance of Taddeo, the young man who served as night clerk when Massimo was off duty, carried him to his room. Disgusted, Feraci went to his own room and put on his pajamas. Gloria was already under the covers, reading, with glasses on her nose. "The food was good, wasn't it?" she asked.

Feraci didn't know what to tell her. In truth, he couldn't remember what he'd eaten. All through the meal, he'd been concentrating on what he'd say to Klemper in the morning; he'd been devising a speech of such authority that every syllable would contain within it an ultimatum. The speech continued to formulate itself even after Feraci had switched off the lights. He couldn't sleep; the darkness around him seemed infinite. He was glad when dawn began to seep through the slats of his shutters. He waited for the smell of morning coffee, imagining how he would be drawn irresistibly toward it, as he was every day; but, instead, it was a loud crash in the lobby that got him out of bed and into his robe.

As it turned out, the crash had been caused by a falling suitcase—Klemper's. Sprung open, it rested on the lobby floor. Klemper knelt next to it, stuffing clothes back in. He looked refreshed.

"Good morning, Signore," he said cheerfully. "I am getting an early start for the trip home."

Ah yes, thought Feraci, the usual evasiveness. "You had a nice time last night?" he asked.

"Very nice," said Klemper. "It was a lovely party. I have given Taddeo some extra money to pay for the restaurant bill."

Taddeo, behind the desk, smiled and waved a wad of lire.

"Herr Klemper," said Feraci, "as you surely know, there is something we must discuss."

"In a minute." Klemper sat on the suitcase to close it. Then, grunting, he grabbed it by the handle and set it right. *"Oof,"* he said, breathing hard. "I should take more exercise." He straightened up and rubbed the small of his back. "Did I mention at dinner that I am thinking about doing something new on my next vacation?"

"You didn't mention," Feraci said. He was distracted, half awake. The text of his speech was no longer so clear to him, and he was trying to recall it.

"Perhaps I may go to Wyoming, in America."

"Wyoming? What's in Wyoming?"

"Dude ranch."

"You want to be a cowboy?" Feraci asked.

"You don't think I'd make a good one?"

"I don't know," Feraci said, further confused by the image of Klemper on horseback.

Klemper laughed. "Well, Signore," he said, "again it is time for goodbye. I have had a fine stay." He hugged Feraci and shook hands with Taddeo, ran a finger along the top of the desk. "No dust. *Bravo*." Feraci trailed him to the elevator and watched him cram his bags inside. Once more, he tried to speak, but the words wouldn't come. The elevator door began to close. "If I go to Wyoming, I'll send you a postcard," Klemper said. *"Arrivederci."* He waved, and then he was gone.

That was the last that Feraci saw of Wilhelm Klemper. He didn't know if Klemper really went to Wyoming, because he never received a postcard. For a while, the month of October spooked him; he couldn't answer the phone without expecting to hear Klemper's voice. No such phone call ever came, but Feraci remained suspicious. He was certain that Klemper must be in the city somewhere, for an attachment to Florence was not so easy to break. After a few years, though, his suspicions began to fade, and his recollections of Klemper became oddly pleasant. Klemper's awful behavior, seen at a distance, seemed more humorous than disastrous, and Feraci often told stories about him to new guests, as a way to make them feel comfortable.

There were other changes as well. As Feraci approached seventy, he took less and less interest in the Ghiberti, preferring to turn the running of it over to Gloria, who thrived on the activity. Massimo showed no interest in helping her; instead of participating in the business, he got a job with a big manufacturer in Milan. His salary was not exceptional, but he had many fringe benefits, including a company car.

So Feraci inherited the little Fiat with the dented fender. The pride he took in learning to drive it was quite extraordinary. Nothing made him happier than to tool around the hills, looking at the city below him. Often, he carried in his pocket the marble toe that Klemper had given him. He knew by now that it had not been chipped from any famous, or even semi-famous, statue, but he thought that someday he might accidentally discover where it belonged and put it back in place. He had no idea if he would need mortar to do the job, or if in fact the job could be done at all, but the question (and others like it) kept him occupied for hours at a time. When he returned to the hotel in the evenings, he spoke of sunsets, of flowing gold.

WHERE THE
MOUNTAINS ARE

ANDERSON sat in the airport lounge in Idaho Falls, reading a technical report and waiting anxiously for his mother's plane to land. Around him, a few country people dressed in cotton Western shirts and denim were sipping Cokes, and one of them remarked rather loudly that the incoming flight had been delayed. So Anderson exchanged his glass of club soda for a bourbon-and-water. He did this with some hesitation, because his mother was a devout Baptist and the slightest tendency toward excess brought a scowl to her face. He had not seen her for almost five years, since an unfortunate scene at his father's funeral, and he was hoping this time not to offend her, to prove himself worthy of her love.

When Mrs. Forché—she'd remarried after Anderson's father died—entered the terminal, however, she seemed not to notice anything, except the temperateness of the air. She wore a heavy tweed suit with a silver armadillo pinned to the collar. She was seventy-three and moved with great vitality, which she credited to a series of stretching exercises that a visiting minister had demonstrated at her church in Houston.

"Why, this is not bad at all!" she exclaimed, taking hold of Anderson's arm. "It must be eighty degrees!"

"It's June, Mom." Anderson kissed her cheek, and discovered that she still used the same creamy makeup base she'd used when he was a kid. "Almost July."

"I know what month it is," said Mrs. Forché. "But the West is so unpredictable. It could have been snowing!" She slipped off her white gloves, and peered into the crowd. "Where's Arthur Earl?" she asked.

Arthur Earl, Anderson's only child, was about to graduate from high school. This grand event had occasioned Mrs. Forché's trip; it had also provoked Anderson's spirit of reconciliation.

"Graduation practice," Anderson said, lying.

"You'd think he'd skip it to meet his grandmother."

"He couldn't. It was required."

"I'll bet he came out to meet Carol's mother," said Mrs. Forché.

"She doesn't get here until tomorrow. Listen, I have to warn you about something, Mom. Arthur Earl doesn't want to be called Arthur Earl anymore."

"Why ever not?" Mrs. Forché said. Arthur Earl had been named in honor of her late husband.

Anderson shrugged. "He says it makes him feel like a redneck."

"Redneck?" said Mrs. Forché in disbelief. "Why, that name has a history." She peeled off the jacket of her suit, as if preparing to do battle. "What does he *want* to be called?"

"Ted."

"*Ted?* Isn't that a sissy name?"

"Not in Idaho," Anderson said. "He's just going through a stage. He'll get over it."

Mrs. Forché wrinkled her nose and sniffed at her son's breath. "What have you been drinking, Buddy?" she asked.

"I had a bourbon while I was waiting for you," Anderson said, recoiling.

"Well, I'm not going to make a big deal out of it," said Mrs. Forché. "It doesn't do any good to lecture a man your age."

Anderson—known to everybody else in the world as Robert—was forty-seven, although he looked much younger because of his thick black hair. He worked as a technical writer for Arkton Industrials, a consulting firm dependent on government contracts for its survival. This was not what he'd planned to do with his life. He had wanted to be a real writer, and had actually published a number of promising stories in little magazines during the late fifties, when he'd resided in Paris and earned his keep, like James Joyce before him, teaching English to upwardly mobile merchants and their daughters. He had married one such daughter, then lived for a while at her father's country house in Gironde composing a serious novel, until the daughter left him for a filthy mechanic whose only passion was riding his motorbike through the vineyards at a murderous clip.

He met Carol, his present wife, on the rebound. She was traveling across Europe with a college study group, but her interest in academic matters faded when she saw Anderson, in his beret and navy-blue turtleneck, making journal entries at a café table. "Nobody cares about art," he told her moodily over a half liter of vin ordinaire. Over the second half liter, he shouted, "But art has the power to unify!" Over the third, he invited her back to his so-called studio, a cold, bathless hotel room in which a well-thumbed copy of *Ulysses* served as central icon, and showed her stacks of manuscript and fumbled badly with the buttons on her dress.

They were wed in August of the following year, and departed immediately for San Francisco, where they stayed for almost a decade. Anderson paid the rent on a small apartment near Golden Gate Park by selling free-lance articles to every magazine and trade journal in the Bay Area. He became an expert in esoteric information—the temperature at which gasoline boils, the capital of Rumania. At night, he labored like a jeweler on one or another of his novels—many were in progress now. Perhaps he could have continued in this fashion forever, but Arthur Earl kept growing and his future had to be considered. What if he wanted to go to college someday? How could they possibly afford it? Anderson was thrown into a turmoil of guilt, during which he alienated most of his friends by confessing, over and over again, that he'd been a bad provider. He looked everywhere for a steady job, but had no success until he attended, in desperation, a widely advertised recruitment seminar sponsored by Arkton Industrials. The seminar was held at the downtown Hilton, and Anderson, billing himself as an industrialist manqué, spent hours in the hospitality suite, talking baseball with a good old boy from Galveston, who happened also to be an Arkton vice-president.

A month later, Anderson was living in Idaho Falls, wearing polyester shirts and commuting daily to a huge, wedge-shaped building on the outskirts of town. He so enjoyed the novelty of a regular paycheck that all thoughts of Joyce, and the unifying power of art, were banished from his mind. He learned to cut his own firewood, change the points and plugs on a three-quarter-ton pickup, to bowl, square dance, ski, and fly-fish. On warm summer evenings, like those that were just beginning, he bolted from the office at five and drove out to a fast-flowing creek that most locals avoided because of its rattlesnake population. Occasionally, he persuaded Arthur Earl to come along, and together they fished the riffles, using elk-hair caddis flies to attract rainbow and cutthroat trout. They always stopped in the little town of Bone on their way home. From the porch of the general store, they watched the sun drop behind the hills, and then watched the surrounding wheat fields and cattle ranches turn a dusky shade of purple. Anderson drank beer, so cold it numbed his tongue. Usually, Arthur Earl had a 7-Up, but on a recent night he'd asked for a Coors. After a moment's hesitation, Anderson said, "Sure, why not?" and plunked down seventy-five cents with such confidence that he felt, for the first time, exactly like a father.

It was this newfound sense of maturity that Anderson wished to demonstrate to his own mother. He was proud of his house, the first he'd ever bought. Big and green, it occupied a large corner lot and had a redwood deck in the back yard, from which you could see the outlying mountains.

"Guess what it cost me," he asked, parking in the driveway.

"Oh, I wouldn't have any idea," said Mrs. Forché. She wished that her new husband, who had a head for figures, was with her.

"C'mon, take a guess."

"Eighty thousand?"

Anderson laughed—he was preening. "Sixty-two five," he said. "And that included the power mower."

"I'd say you got yourself a real bargain," Mrs. Forché said, although, in truth, the house seemed boxy and awkward to her, lacking in the stout-hearted landscaping—broad-needled pines and luxuriant St. Augustine grass—that made the suburbs of Houston so comforting.

Carol stood in the doorway, waving. She was a thin, virtuous woman, who'd developed a bad habit of biting her fingernails during the lean San Francisco years. Her lingering fear of poverty had caused her to take a part-time job as a typist for a local manufacturer. She spoke seldom, but she always had something to say.

"How was your flight?" she asked, depositing Mrs. Forché's cosmetics case on a table.

"We were delayed for an hour in Salt Lake," said Mrs. Forché. "I ate a sandwich and read the Psalms."

In the bathroom, Mrs. Forché freshened up. She took off her nylons, marveling at the heat, then splashed some water on her cheeks and set off on an exploratory tour of the house. She peeked into the guest bedroom, where her luggage was stored, and into the master bedroom. Then she peeked into the third bedroom and found Arthur Earl. He was stretched out on his bed, with headphones shielding his ears, reading a Stephen King novel. He didn't seem to recognize his grandmother when he looked up.

"Yes, it's me, all right," she said brightly.

Arthur Earl blinked his heavy lids. He removed the headphones and placed them carefully on a pillow.

"Have you got a kiss for me?" Mrs. Forché asked. "How did your practice go?"

"Practice?"

Anderson appeared in the room, transported magically from the kitchen. "Graduation practice," he said, winking above his mother's blue-gray hair. "You must have finished early."

"We must have," said Arthur Earl.

He rolled off the bed. At six foot three, he was five inches taller than Anderson, and seemed to have extra arms and legs. There were gaping holes in his socks.

"I thought I told you to throw those out," Anderson said in annoyance.

"Well, you *didn't* tell me," said Arthur Earl, contorting his face as if Anderson had accused him of a heinous crime. "Maybe you *thought* you told me, but you didn't." He exhibited a naked toe. "Anyway, they're not so terrible."

"Just cut the crap," said Anderson in disgust.

Arthur Earl kissed his grandmother. She seemed to float up into his extra arms. When he set her down, she patted his shoulder and stared knowingly at him.

"I can see Grandpa in your eyes," she said. "You resemble him, Arthur Earl."

"I wish you wouldn't call me that." He put a hand on his hip and turned toward Anderson. "You were *supposed* to explain, Dad."

"I did explain. Grandma probably forgot."

But Mrs. Forché had not forgotten. She grabbed Arthur

Earl by his T-shirt sleeve and adopted an inquisitional tone. "Why would you want to change your name, boy? What kind of a name is Ted, anyhow?"

"I like it better, is all," he said.

"I certainly don't," said Mrs. Forché. "I don't like it a bit."

Arthur Earl chewed on his lip, in an effort to be polite. "I'm sorry you don't, Grandma," he said. "But it's my life. I'm the one who has to live it." He turned to his father. "Give me the keys to the truck, will you?"

"What for?"

"I want to get it washed."

"You have a date?" Anderson asked coyly.

"None of your business," said Arthur Earl, sounding pressed. "I have some very important errands to do tomorrow. So just hand 'em over."

As soon as the keys touched his palm, he vanished. Some music seeped out of his headphones.

He did not return in time for dinner, so they ate without him, grouped around a wrought-iron table on the deck. Anderson prevailed upon his mother to have a taste of wine. She avoided the offering for a few minutes, then began to sip delicately at it, hummingbird style. It went right to her head and added to the surprising sensation of warmth and well-being that had attended her since arrival. It seemed odd to her now that the prospect of the trip had once filled her with dread.

"That Arthur Earl," she said, eyes flashing, "he takes after you, Buddy. He's such a feisty child!"

She told Carol how Anderson had run away from home when he was ten, and then again when he was twelve, managing to jump a freight the second time and ride it all the way to Beaumont, before he got scared and turned himself in at the police station. His father, an explosive hardware salesman who chain-smoked Luckies, had to drive for hours through a miserable hailstorm to claim him, and afterward their battling, which was already fierce, became more intense than ever. They clashed over the most insignificant things—a scrap of meat left on a plate, the distance the family Buick should be parked from the curb. Mrs. Forché, asked to choose sides, chose her husband's. She had never really got close to Buddy, not even later, when he was a young man brimming with enthusiasm for literature, actively seeking her approval. She just didn't understand him. The magazines he sent her from Paris were upsetting. What pleasure could she derive from seeing the name Anderson sandwiched between vulgar words and pen-and-ink drawings of naked women? She stuffed them in a bottom drawer and never mentioned them to anybody. Instead, she explained her son's wandering by inventing stories of her own—Buddy translating articles for the American consul, Buddy teaching the children of diplomats at an exclusive school on the Champs-Élysées.

She expected him to begin an intelligible career when he settled in San Francisco with his new wife, but he acted more scattered than he had in Europe. He had no sense of responsibility. He dressed like a bum and mailed her pamphlets criticizing the government. There was a nasty scene in Houston, when he came to his father's funeral in blue jeans, with hair down to his shoulders and a wispy little psychopath's mustache on his upper lip. "Don't you have any respect for the dead?" she shouted at him, refusing to believe that he hadn't meant to insult or offend her, that instead he had boarded the plane in a condition of obliterative rage, wishing he could raise up the old man and forgive him for everything. She wouldn't answer his letters, even the apologetic ones, for months after. They were beautiful letters, she had to admit, full of poetry, but all the poetry on earth wasn't going to feed poor Arthur Earl, or put something other than ventilated sneakers on his feet. So she was glad when Buddy gave up his literary quest, and near to ecstasy when he accepted the job in Idaho Falls. Already she could tell that the acquisition of some basic American household goods—a couch, a guest bed, a toaster oven—had altered the texture of Buddy's marriage. He no longer picked at Carol; there was a bit of fat under his chin.

After eating, Mrs. Forché felt tired and went to her room. She put on her nightgown, sat on the rug, and performed a few of her exercises. But an irresistible weariness soon came over her, and, gradually, she was drawn into bed. She could hear Arthur Earl laughing at the television set, downstairs in the family room. This gave her a feeling of continuity—children in their secret places. She tried to read her Bible, but she couldn't concentrate. Mountains, in all their spatial wonder, kept impinging on her mind.

In the morning, Anderson drove to the airport to meet Mrs. Whiting, Carol's mother. He was somewhat in awe of her; she had a toughness that intimidated him. Her ex-husband, a stockbroker with whom he'd once played a duffer's round of golf, called her Sister Impenetrable, which wasn't fair, really, because she was open and generous and had come to Anderson's financial assistance on several occasions. His acocunt with her was still slightly in arrears.

She was the first one off the plane and carried a large, gaudily wrapped package. "You would not believe what happened to me on the way to Kennedy," she said, striding briskly toward the baggage-claim area. "A terrorist tried to steal my taxi! At least, I thought he was a terrorist. You know the type—beady eyes, a dirty raincoat?" She stopped to adjust her slip. "Anyway, there we were, parked on Third, when this little terrorist jumps into the back seat and orders the driver to take him to the West Side. I nearly died!" she said. "Fortunately, he was unarmed. In fact, he had a screw loose. But we couldn't get him out of the cab. He just sat there mumbling, 'West Side, West Side.' Finally, the driver flagged down a cop. Then it was good-bye, little terrorist. I was sure I'd miss my flight." Suddenly she quit talking and gave Anderson a military peck on the cheek. "Be a dear, Robert, and help me with this stuff."

Mrs. Whiting, who lived in Manhattan and considered herself something of an urban guerrilla, had visited Idaho Falls twice before, and consequently she entered Anderson's house with a tremendous lack of ceremony. She dropped her bags in the living room, poured herself an iced tea, and perched on a wicker stool in the kitchen, waiting for Carol to return from work. When the front door opened a bit later, she shouted, "In here, dear!" but instead of her daughter she saw a small, bright-eyed woman in a Houston Oilers sweatshirt.

"This is my mom," Anderson said. "Gertrude Forché, Louise Whiting."

Mrs. Forché was breathing hard. She clasped Mrs. Whiting's hand in hers. "Pardon my sweat," she said. "I was out for my walk."

"I used to go walking all the time," said Mrs. Whiting, "until I got bursitis in my knee."

"I know some good exercises for joint problems," said Mrs. Forché.

Both women were lying on the rug when Carol got home.

"I can't get up right now," Mrs. Whiting yelled, throwing a kiss. "I'm learning to cure myself."

"She's much more dexterous than she thought," said Mrs. Forché.

"Watch how this leg bends!"

Carol observed the bending of the leg, smiling wryly. Nothing her mother did came as a surprise anymore. "Robert," she said, surveying the clutter in the living room, "why is Mom's luggage all over everywhere?"

"Haven't had a chance to take it downstairs yet," Anderson said.

Mrs. Forché, still supine, registered an objection. "Those steps would be murder on her knee," she said. "You move my things down there, Buddy."

"Don't be silly, Gertrude." Mrs. Whiting pressed her diaphragm with her fingertips. "I have steps in my apartment building and manage them just fine."

"But it's no *bother* to me," Mrs. Forché insisted. "We'll switch and that's that."

Further argument was curtailed when the phone rang. It was Arthur Earl, calling from a gas station near Ashton, forty miles away, where the pickup had broken down.

"What the hell were you doing in *Ashton*?" Anderson asked angrily.

"I gave this girl a ride up there to her uncle's house. She missed her bus."

"I'll bet."

"Listen, Dad," said Arthur Earl. "You don't have to believe me if you don't want to. But it's not my fault the damn truck doesn't run right. The mechanic, he said the oil hadn't been changed for probably ten thousand miles."

Anderson knew this was true. He modulated his voice in order to make a request. "How'd you feel about sleeping downstairs in the family room for a couple nights?"

"Forget it."

"That means I'll have to put Grandma Forché down there."

"I'd do it any other time," Arthur Earl said. "*Any* other time. But not now. Not with graduation coming."

"Thanks, sport," said Anderson.

Anderson transferred his mother's bags while Mrs. Whiting chatted on the phone. He felt awful about it. The family room was damp and moldy and decorated with wine-spattered posters from the old Fillmore auditorium. An upright piano, its keys frigid to the touch, was shoved against the far wall. On top of it rested a rubber Richard Nixon mask that Anderson used to wear at political rallies. He put it on and opened his arms wide in a gesture of embrace.

"Welcome to Siberia, Mom," he said.

But Mrs. Forché wasn't paying attention. Instead, she was testing one of her favorite Sunday-school lessons: trying to make the best of things.

"I guess this must pull out into a bed," she said, examining a worn purple couch. "It's nice and comfortable." Then her eyes encountered a patch of dried orange matter, and she balked. "There's a pretty bad stain on this cushion, Buddy," she said.

Anderson, mask in hand, investigated. "It's that cheese junk Arthur Earl sprays on crackers," he said bitterly. "I'll probably need a blowtorch to get it off." He flopped onto the couch and tugged at his beard. "I'm sorry about this, Mom," he said. "It never occurred to us, about her knee. We've never *had* more than one guest before."

"You're getting yourself worked up over nothing," said Mrs. Forché.

Anderson had heard this sentence maybe eight million times. In the past, it had always been addressed to his father.

"I'm *not* worked up," he protested. "It's just that I wanted things to be perfect."

"They *are* perfect. Besides, this is only for a day or two. Louise goes back to New York on Sunday."

"That's right," said Anderson, taking consolation where he could.

"Let's make the best of it," said Mrs. Forché.

"I've got a little space heater I'll bring down," said Anderson, rising.

"Quit *worrying* about me now," Mrs. Forché scolded. "I'll be plenty cozy here," she said, although in fact she was disconcerted to have surrendered her view of the mountains for one of Jimi Hendrix wreathed in psychedelic flames.

But the splendor of the landscape was redeemed for Mrs. Forché later in the evening, when she saw the Snake River coursing through downtown Idaho Falls and observed the cleanliness of Mormon architecture; there was a temple as white as the salt of the Great Salt Lake. She was impressed, too, by the restaurant where Anderson took everybody— except Arthur Earl, who was still stranded in Ashton—for dinner. It had a cathedral ceiling inset with stained-glass windows, and plants grew so lushly in the dining room that Mrs. Forché seemed always to be peering around leaves. The waiter was young and handsome and introduced himself as Bob. After dinner, Mrs. Forché popped a peppermint into her mouth and linked her arm through Anderson's for a stroll. At a variety store, she twirled around a postcard rack and asked her son, who was intimate with art, to help her select a few extraordinary panoramas to send to her friends in Houston. She liked especially a packet depicting the natural wonders of Yellowstone Park: eagles, cataracts, geysers.

"The last time we camped at Yellowstone, a bear almost got us," Anderson told her.

"You're kidding!"

"No, I'm not. He came right up and scratched at the truck windows. We were sleeping in back. Ask Arthur Earl about it. He's the one who forgot to put the food away."

Mrs. Forché studied a tinted photo of deer browsing on a ridge. "I'd like to go there someday. I don't believe we have anything like it in Texas."

Ultimately, she bought four packets, along with a funny graduation card in which she planned to enclose a check for Arthur Earl.

"Do you think fifty dollars would be too much?" she asked.

"Far, far too much," said Anderson, thinking about his poor abused truck.

At home, Mrs. Whiting suggested a nightcap. Mrs.

Forché, elevating an eyebrow, did not partake; in her opinion, Mrs. Whiting had just crossed a subtle line. She was becoming rather critical of the New York woman, who talked too much and mistook pushiness for energy. Instead of joining the others in the living room, Mrs. Forché sat by herself at the kitchen table, soberly studying Yellowstone, its glories and dangers. The effort to encompass the park with her imagination began to exhaust her, and she was about to retire, when Mrs. Whiting, whose cheeks were inflamed with Kahlúa, begged Carol to play a few songs on the piano.

Carol knew it was useless to argue; after a certain point, her mother's demands were non-negotiable. She led the company downstairs, then played "Raindrops Keep Fallin' on My Head." She played "Unchained Melody" and the theme from "Moulin Rouge." Then she played some Mozart.

"Play 'Clair de Lune,' " said Mrs. Whiting in a husky voice. "You *know* how I love it!"

Carol was playing Scott Joplin rags when Arthur Earl came clumping down the steps, shortly after midnight. He had a goofy expression on his face.

"Nice of you to stop by," Anderson said. "Is the truck okay?"

"Truck's fine," said Arthur Earl, scratching his nose. "It's sleeping."

"Always a joke," said Anderson.

"Oh, Robert," said Mrs. Whiting. "Leave him alone. He's practically a grown man."

"*All right*, Grandma!" cried Arthur Earl. "Hey, did you try the buffalo-meat chili? Was it great, or was it great?"

Mrs. Whiting looked perplexed. "Buffalo-meat chili?"

"Didn't you take them to Lester's Cafeteria, Dad?" Arthur Earl wailed. "You were supposed to take 'em to Lester's."

"We had steaks instead. Plain broiled steaks," Anderson told him. "Where did you eat?"

"The girl's uncle, he fried up some trout he got at Henry's Fork. Hey, check these out!"

Arthur Earl reached into his shirt pocket, then dumped a handful of tiny blue-winged flies on the piano top.

Anderson inspected them for craftsmanship. "The uncle tied these?" he asked.

Before Arthur Earl could answer, Carol said, "Where did your mother go, Robert?"

They found her upstairs, napping on the living-room couch, a borrowed ski parka covering her legs and her postcard packet shielding her eyes from the light.

On graduation morning, Anderson, in his bathrobe, watched his mother, who'd awakened early, setting the table for breakfast. She moved stiffly. Her housecoat, pink and flowered, was wrinkled in places, and Anderson thought he could see imprinted on it the lumps of the mattress on which she'd been forced to sleep. From the guest room, in contrast, came the imperturbable snoring of Mrs. Whiting.

Arthur Earl bounded to the table. He threw a leg over a chair back and let himself sink into a seat.

"What's this?" he asked, reaching for an envelope propped against the saltshaker.

"A little something for you," said Mrs. Forché.

Arthur Earl smiled and attacked the envelope. He made a big show of reading the card inside before looking at the check.

"Fifty dollars!" he whooped. "You must be crazy!" He caught himself. "I don't mean crazy—I mean, you know, *thanks!*" Then he looked at Mrs. Forché and seemed to realize for the first time how old she was—her hands, as she mixed the pancake batter, were like claws. "But really, Grandma," he said, very solemnly, "I can't take this. It's too much. You need it."

"If I needed it, I wouldn't have given it to you," said Mrs. Forché. "So just hush your mouth and go spend it on something wild."

For Arthur Earl, the whole day was like this, lit with potency and recognitions. When he put on his new blue shirt, his baby fat seemed to disappear, and he acquired an elegant taper of the sort he had long imagined would accompany the onset of maturity. At school, he covered the shirt with a graduation gown, but even this obligatory nod in the direction of uniformity did not diminish his shapeliness. His body felt light and airy. He joined the other graduates in a line that stretched from the football team's locker room to a point near the main parking lot, and stood next to his friend Terry Andrews, a mole-faced boy who was intensely proud of his parents' wheat farm near Bone. They joked about events that now seemed historical, linked to a past they would not soon forget, but they had to quit when the impassioned baton of Mr. Dante Ferrigno led the school band into the initial chords of "Pomp and Circumstance."

Moving forward, Arthur Earl was gripped by unexpected emotion. The band's brass section, always notorious for its tinniness, roared in his ears. He walked through the goalposts and across the ten-yard line, keeping his eyes on the worn green grass, so he wouldn't start crying. But then he saw the bare feet of the girl marching ahead of him, which made him giggle audibly and poke Terry Andrews in the ribs. He bet Andrews a dollar that the principal would use the word "responsibility" at least five times in his speech. He won. He felt prescient and gazed toward the distant bleachers, certain that he could divine the figures of his family in the otherwise undifferentiated mass of flesh.

They were there, of course—Anderson and Carol and the two grandmothers, both of whom had dressed in shades of red so vivid that they obliterated the delicate orchid corsages Anderson had ordered from the florist. Mrs. Whiting had already removed her corsage, because it irritated the membranes of her nose. Presently, she was complaining to Carol about the hardness of the bleacher slats, which had caused a numbness in her bottom. As usual, Carol only half listened to the complaints, preferring instead to observe the ceremony and fan her face with a rolled-up graduation program. It was the program that had most bothered Mrs. Forché—or more accurately, that had served as the focus of her many discontents. She could not understand how Arthur Earl had chosen to list himself as Ted, especially on such a formal occasion. She interpreted it as an act of betrayal, which went against every notion of justice she'd ever entertained.

"I'm glad his granddaddy's not alive to witness this," she whispered to Anderson. "That boy needs a haircut, too!"

Anderson ignored her. Graduation had filled him with a devout, if predictable, sadness, which pursued him onto the field when the ceremony ended and made him stumble, like an elderly pensioner, over slippery heaps of discarded caps and gowns. Finally, he found Arthur Earl—huge, beaming—among the others and congratulated him as best he could, but he was overwhelmed by the strength he felt emanating from his son. His melancholy deepened when Arthur Earl introduced him to a raven-haired girl from Ashton, whose ecstatic beauty seemed not really vivifying but as perishable as orchids.

The family rode home in silence, then went about preparing for Arthur Earl's party. Anderson, still in a black mood, opened a bottle of champagne and reflected on how the cork echoed hollowly down the hallway, presaging centuries of emptiness. Carol set out a buffet of cold cuts, cheese, bread, and salads, which waited in compositional isolation, preserved under Saran Wrap, for Arthur Earl and his pals, who arrived only twenty minutes later than they'd promised and devoured most of the food before Mrs. Forché, in an ill-fitting apron, could pour them some punch.

"Hey!" shouted Arthur Earl, heading for the stereo. "We need music!"

"Wait, wait, *wait!*" cried Mrs. Whiting, rising spiritedly from the couch, where she'd been drinking champagne and discussing wheat futures with Terry Andrews. She returned from the guest room with the large package she'd brought from New York. It was another gift for Arthur Earl—an expensive portable radio whose miniaturized speakers afforded the utmost in fidelity to the listener.

"This must have cost a fortune," Terry Andrews sighed,

lying on the rug so he could scrutinize the elaborate dials and gauges more closely.

Mrs. Forché knelt beside him; the radio made her check seem insignificant. "It's even got shortwave," she said.

"Let's fire it up, Grandma," said Arthur Earl, tuning in some hard rock and snapping his fingers gleefully. But Anderson intervened and switched to a compromise station that played more placid music. He started the dancing by whisking Carol around the room in an exaggerated foxtrot. He held her tightly, recalling Paris and the erstwhile sexual energy that had resulted in Arthur Earl. Dancing next with the raven-haired girl, he watched the movement of her hips to see if she was a virgin. Next, he asked his mother to dance, performing a few funny steps to entice her.

"You stink of champagne," she said, scowling. "You smell like you fell into a vat."

"Relax, Mom," he said. "This happens once in a life-time." He kept dancing by himself, feeling better now.

After a while, Mrs. Forché said, "I think fifty dollars is plenty to give to a young boy, don't you?"

"I sure do. Besides, Arthur Earl would rather have money than anything."

"That's what *I* thought," said Mrs. Forché, adjusting her glasses. "She"—nodding at Mrs. Whiting—"is just show-ing off."

"I don't think she meant to."

"Well, you don't know her like I do. I've been keeping an eye on her. She can be wicked."

"Come on and dance," Anderson said. He was doing a variation of the Twist.

"I will *not* dance with a fool!" shouted Mrs. Forché.

Anderson had forgotten how nasty she could be when hurt. She chewed on a fingernail and tried to compose herself.

"I'm sorry, Buddy," she said. "I don't feel too well."

"You're probably tired. It's been a long day."

Mrs. Forché confessed that she hadn't slept at all the night before. "It's chilly down there, even with the heater."

"I'll put some extra blankets on the bed," Anderson said.

"I doubt they'll help," Mrs. Forché said. She dabbed at her nose with a Kleenex she kept stored in the sleeve of her blouse. "That draft, it goes right through me."

"We'll fix it for you."

But Mrs. Forché had turned away to stare in awe at Mrs. Whiting, who was dancing animatedly with Terry Andrews, moving with surprising grace.

"You see, Buddy?" she said. "There's nothing wrong with that woman. She's as nimble as I am!"

"She's feeling loose, Mom."

"Don't give me that," Mrs. Forché said contemptuously. "The woman's wicked, all right—she tricked me out of the good bedroom."

As if cursed by this harsh accusation, Mrs. Whiting lost her balance quite suddenly, clutched at her bad knee, and dropped like a deadweight to the floor.

It was only a mild ankle sprain, the doctor said. He prescribed three days' bed rest, followed by a week on crutches.

"What a stupid thing to do!" Mrs. Whiting said. She was lying regally on the guest bed, surrounded by the family, plus Terry Andrews, who felt so bad about the accident that he kept stuffing fresh ice cubes into the ice pack on Mrs. Whiting's head. "I had no business dancing! No business whatsoever!"

"You were celebrating," said Mrs. Forché, who was sunk in her own apocalyptic version of guilt.

"That's no excuse. A person with my medical history should *not* have been on the dance floor." She motioned Mrs. Forché to her bedside. "Gertrude, this is so awful for you. I know what a difficult time you've been having downstairs."

"Difficult?" asked Mrs. Forché. "Why, it hasn't been difficult at all!"

Arthur Earl spoke up. "Anyway, she can have my bed, now that graduation's over."

"No need for that," said Anderson. "We're going to take a trip to Yellowstone."

This came as a surprise to Mrs. Forché. At first, she refused to go. She was very tired, and her sniffling was much worse. But Anderson wore her down: Hadn't she expressed a deep admiration for Yellowstone? Wouldn't she like to spend a night or two in the wonderful lodge there? How many chances would she have to visit the park, especially in company with her only son?

So the next morning, grumbling a little, Mrs. Forché dressed in her tweed suit, swallowed an antihistamine, packed a small bag with essentials, and joined Anderson in the cab of the pickup truck. She sat on an embroidered pillow, which permitted her to see over the dashboard and observe their gradual ascent into the mountains. She was still tired; her bones ached with apprehension.

About forty miles from Idaho Falls, Henry's Fork of the Snake River came into view. It was a slow-flowing band of glistening water, over which insects sailed in great profusion. Anderson passed several fishermen before giving in to temptation and pulling to the side of the road.

"Why are we stopping?" asked Mrs. Forché. "Is something wrong?"

"Nothing's wrong," Anderson said. "I want to fish for a minute or two."

His mother frowned. She studied the map, using her fingers like calipers to measure distances.

"It's still a long way to Yellowstone," she said. "It won't be any fun if we get there after dark."

Anderson had already assembled his rod. "Plenty of time, Mom," he said, starting for the river.

Mrs. Forché trailed him, throwing his down jacket over her shoulders as added protection against the chill in the air. She perched on a tree stump and watched him sift through the pine needles and organic debris at the river's edge.

"What ever are you looking for?" she asked, zipping up the jacket.

"Insect casings. The bugs shed them as they grow."

"Is that your bait?"

"No, but what I find tells me what the trout are eating. I try to match the natural with an imitation. Some of these bugs, they have a brief life cycle."

This reminded Mrs. Forché of a sermon on cosmic time she'd heard one Sunday. "What seems brief to you might be forever to them," she said.

"I won't argue with that." Anderson tied on a tiny blue fly.

"Do you ever think about your daddy anymore?"

Anderson considered the question. For a minute, he

thought of lying, but then he told the truth. "Not very often," he said. "On his birthday, maybe. Or around the holidays, when we all used to be together. But the memories are very intense, you know? Almost like electric shocks."

"Isn't that odd?" said Mrs. Forché. "I feel his presence constantly. It must be different for the children."

"What's odd to me," said Anderson, "is that the memories never make me sad." He smiled and waded into the river, casting to rising fish. In a half hour, he hooked only one small rainbow, which he held aloft for his mother's approval before releasing it.

"That's a pretty fish! Have you noticed those clouds, Buddy?" She pointed to some dark thunderheads on the horizon.

"We're practically in Big Sky Country," Anderson said jovially. "Those clouds blow through all the time."

"I don't want to get trapped in a storm!"

"You won't get trapped," said Anderson, picking up slack line.

Moments later, the clouds opened and rain fell in thick sheets. Mrs. Forché covered her head with the jacket and walked away at a brisk pace, scratching her legs on the underbrush. Anderson was drenched when he got to the truck; water coursed down his cheeks and dripped onto the seats.

"Are you okay?" he asked.

"Oh, I'm fine," said Mrs. Forché. "But I tore my hose all to pieces." She plucked sorrowfully at the runs in her stockings. "I can't go into any hotel looking like this."

Anderson turned the heater up full blast. "I wish I had

a little whiskey to give you," he said. "For medicinal purposes. Like they do in the Alps."

"I'd sooner freeze," said Mrs. Forché.

It did not stop raining until just before they drove
through the park gates. By then, they were no longer on
speaking terms. Mrs. Forché was sniffling loudly, extracting
one Kleenex after another from her sleeve, while Anderson
surreptitiously probed the itchy skin rash forming under
his damp jeans.

He tried to interest his mother in an osprey circling
above the Madison River, but it held no more fascination
for her than a common vulture might. The pluming
geysers near the Firehole also left her cold. Even a herd of
elk grazing in a meadow failed to rouse her; she thought
they looked ordinary when compared to the pictures on her
postcards. But Yellowstone wasn't really to blame—she was
simply too bone-weary to appreciate it. It made her feel
insignificant, dominated by things beyond her control. She
was homesick for the flatlands of Houston.

All this was evident to Anderson, who'd been captured
by a gloom far more insidious than the melancholy he'd
experienced during graduation. With Arthur Earl, he had
years left, if he was lucky, but his mother was fading from
him and he had not yet touched her in any essential way.
The many errors that now seemed to compose the fabric
of his life rose before him, and he surrendered briefly to
the self-pity that had governed his sentimental youth.

"Buddy," said Mrs. Forché, shivering inside the down
jacket, "I've seen enough for today."

He took her to the park lodge and led her to a chair by
the huge stone fireplace, in which a fire was burning. Then

he went to the registration desk and received another severe disappointment—there were no reservations in the name of Anderson.

"I don't believe this," he groaned. "I phoned early in the morning. I reserved two singles."

"I show no record of it," the clerk said. "It's probably a computer error." She shuffled through some index cards. "But I can give you a nice big room with twins, up on the second floor."

Anderson pleaded his case before the assistant manager, but without success. The lodge was booked solid. So he carried the bags to the room, then helped his mother climb the steps.

"Why, there's two beds in here!" she said.

"We're roommates, Mom," Anderson said. "It's not my fault. The computer made a mistake." He set down his tackle box. "I don't know why the hell they allow computers in national parks."

Mrs. Forché was too tired to become involved in another controversy. She stepped into the bathroom and emerged wearing a long red nightgown.

Anderson was dismayed. "Aren't you hungry? I thought we'd go get something to eat."

"Let's have room service," said Mrs. Forché, who was looking through the bureau drawers.

"They don't have room service."

"Maybe you could bring me something, then. About all I could eat with this cold is a cup of soup, and tea and toast." She got beneath the covers of the bed farthest from the window. "Isn't there supposed to be a Bible in here?" she asked querulously. "Aren't the Gideons supposed to put Bibles everywhere?"

"I'll see if I can find one downstairs."

In the restaurant, Anderson ordered the food, including a hamburger for himself, and told the waitress he'd come back for it in a little while. He walked out onto a terrace, hoping to take solace from the sunset, as he did so often in Bone, but a bitter wind was blowing through the canyon. Even the month of June had let him down; the temperature was thirty-eight degrees.

Inside, he searched for a Bible. There was a small bookcase in an alcove off the lobby, but the only religious item among the condensations and faded mysteries was an essay collection by Norman Vincent Peale. Next to it was a thick, moldy paperback called *The World's Greatest Stories*. He took it down and, sitting by the fire, browsed through the contents. Predictably, he encountered Chesterton, Saki, and O. Henry, but he also found, much to his delight, his favorite Joyce story, which told of the Misses Morkan's annual dance and the secrets revealed during it. Again the words brought an ease to his being, and he was halfway through the text before he remembered his food.

Upstairs, Mrs. Forché was busy draping a blanket over a piece of monofilament fishing line she'd strung between a nail and a curtain rod. She seemed refreshed by her nap; her wispy hair was freshly brushed.

"Just like Clark Gable and Claudette Colbert," she said, accepting the carton of soup and digging right in. She worked her plastic spoon past some limp vegetables and tasted the yellowish broth. Then she frowned. "Buddy, this is barely warm. How am I supposed to eat it?"

Anderson chewed on his hamburger.

"Did you find me a Bible?" his mother asked.

"There weren't any around. I've got something else here I'd like to read you."

"Read me?" She laughed. "I'm not a child." Then she peered at the book in his hand. "What is it?"

"It's a story by James Joyce," he said.

"Oh, I don't like that kind of thing!"

"Now, listen," said Anderson, hearing a bit of his father's outrage creep into his voice. "Don't take that attitude. This is a wonderful story. You're going to love it."

He started to read it aloud, even faking an Irish accent, and after a few paragraphs Mrs. Forché admitted that the story had merit. It was not in the same league as David and Goliath, or Daniel in the lions' den, but it was soothing nonetheless. She finished her tepid soup and returned to the warmth of her covers; in a moment, she was asleep. Anderson, who knew the story by heart, closed the book. He stared at his mother's face, which, in repose, projected a girlish innocence, and then tidied up the blanket separating the beds. He stretched out, fully clothed, and soon he was snoring. Of his dreams, little can be said, but when he woke later and went to the window, the earth, in all its observable latitudes, was dusted with a fine powder of snow.

THE END
OF THE WORLD

THE STORE that sold mission suits was in downtown Salt Lake City. Donald Edmunds, who was about to begin his missionary effort, went there with his mother. "San Francisco, that's where he's going to," she told the salesperson. "I'm glad it's not Burma or someplace like that." The suit she chose for her son was dark brown. It came with a vest and also a pair of lighter-colored trousers. Edmunds had to admit that her taste was excellent. When he tried on the suit at home, it seemed to give him the sort of solid, mature look he had always associated with the elders of the church. He grew quite fond of it, in fact, thinking that it had somehow been meant for him, so he was very upset when, on his scheduled day of departure, he went out to the airport and found that his partner in the missionary effort, Walter Davis, was wearing exactly the same thing.

"Hey, Donald," said Davis, waving as Edmunds approached. "We're twins."

"I'm no twin of yours," Edmunds said. He was furious.

He grabbed Davis by an elbow and pulled him along. "Didn't they tell you I'd already bought the suit?"

"Nobody said anything. They had about ten of them on the rack."

"Did you get those light-colored trousers?" Edmunds asked. When Davis nodded, he said, "Okay, then, here's what you do. You take your suitcase into the men's room and change into them."

"Why should I do that?"

Edmunds stopped short, put his hands on his hips, and blew some aggravated air out of his mouth, the way his old football coach used to. "I guess you think the missionary effort is just a game, Walter," he said.

"I don't think that."

"Well, how do you figure anybody's going to take us seriously if we're both dressed alike?"

Davis thought this over for a minute or two. "All right," he said, "I'll change."

But the new trousers did not produce the effect that Edmunds had hoped for; instead, they made Davis look clownish. As he walked along next to Edmunds, he seemed to be poking fun at the whole concept of a staid brown suit. The trousers—light beige, with tiny checks—undermined the image that Edmunds had so patiently cultivated. They didn't even fit properly. For some reason, they were so big in the waist that Davis had to cinch his belt to the very last hole, which left a long, inappropriate tongue of leather dangling down.

All the way to San Francisco, Edmunds worried about how he was going to explain the suits to Mr. Harvey, the church elder with whom they were to stay. He had never wanted to be paired with Davis in the first place, because

Davis had an unaggressive attitude toward life which would probably affect his ability to bring in converts. It was Edmunds's plan to apply mental toughness to this missionary effort; he wanted to set a record for most converts in a single city.

Mr. Harvey was waiting for them at the baggage-claim area inside the airport terminal. He had an index card pinned to his lapel; he'd printed MORRIS HARVEY on it in block letters. While Davis collected the bags, Edmunds shook Harvey's hand and said, "You're probably wondering about the suits. The thing is, we had a litle mixup. When I told Walter what color to buy, he thought I said dark *brown*. But what I really said was dark *blue*."

"Dark blue," Harvey repeated. "I understand." He led them to a big Buick in the parking garage. He had a quality of deep distress about him; he was terribly gaunt, as though some private sorrow were eating away his flesh. "I want to show you what we're up against," he said once they were all in his car. He took them on a tour of the Tenderloin. It was a district of X-rated movies and adult bookstores, of winos sleeping on beds of broken glass. They saw bums, pimps, muggers, and thieves; they watched in awe as a kid about their own age stuck a needle into his arm and then rolled back his eyes in stunned pleasure. "There's nothing the police can do about it," Harvey informed them sourly. "This is just daily business down here."

Harvey himself lived outside the city, in the suburb of San Mateo. His house had a big front lawn, on which two ceramic dwarfs were resting on their elbows and smoking pipes. He put Edmunds and Davis in a paneled bedroom in the finished basement. Before dinner, they played Ping-

Pong in another basement room with Harvey's adopted son, who was fourteen and would be going on his own missionary effort in a few years. "Wouldn't it be funny if you got sent to Utah?" Davis said with a laugh. Davis had blue eyes behind round steel-rimmed glasses—eyes like lakes or rivers. Mrs. Harvey called everybody to the table. She was a stout woman who was built like a monument. She served meat and potatoes. The milk came in a pitcher. Edmunds's appetite was not very good, on account of the bumpy plane ride, and Davis kept irritating him by wolfing down everything in sight and talking about things that Edmunds felt were insignificant. Finally, he set his napkin next to his plate and said, "You'd think they didn't feed Walter at home."

"It's a compliment to the cook," said Mrs. Harvey.

"I'm feeling a little sick," Edmunds said. "Could I be excused so I can go to bed?"

In the bedroom, Edmunds undressed, got into his pajamas, and hung up his suit, checking it over for lint. He was eager to begin canvassing the city. What he'd seen in the Tenderloin had convinced him that there were thousands of potential converts around. He had never understood why, when the message of the church was so simple and appealing, more people hadn't taken it to heart. You had to wonder if people didn't prefer to live like pigs, if they didn't wallow in filth by choice.

Edmunds was so tired that he drifted right to sleep, but a loud noise woke him in the middle of the night. He flipped on his lamp and saw that Davis was missing from the bed across the room. He walked into the hallway and then toward an open door at its end. The door led into the garage, where Davis was lying on the concrete, touching his fingers to a bruise on his forehead.

"I was looking for the bathroom," Davis told him.

"It's the other way," Edmunds said in disgust. "Why didn't you turn on the light?"

"Couldn't find it."

The garage was filled with cardboard cartons. Each one was marked—powdered milk, sugar, flour, canned goods, freeze-dried meals. Edmunds remembered how at dinner Morris Harvey had said that his family was ready for anything—race war, nuclear war, it didn't matter. "Survival supplies," Edmunds said, sitting on a carton.

"I was having a nightmare, Don." Davis rubbed his bruise. "I kept seeing those faces from this afternoon. But they were more ugly, you know what I mean? I could hear them moaning."

"You ate too much. Didn't I warn you to go slow?"

"I think I'm afraid."

"What are you afraid of?"

Davis shrugged. "I don't know if I can help those people," he said.

"You can help them. You've just got to be tough about it."

"What if the world is coming to an end? I don't want to die."

"The world is *not* coming to an end," Edmunds said. He knew this was true. He went over to Davis; they shared a moment of silent prayer.

In the morning, and every morning after that, Harvey dropped them somewhere in the city on his way to work, and they walked from door to door with leaflets and brochures, trying to spread the message. Edmunds, who had a statistical mind, kept track of their record on a clipboard. It was not very impressive. In their first six weeks, they had eighty-two polite conversations, but a polite conversation could not be counted as a success unless it resulted in some kind of positive commitment, like an invitation into a home or apartment. They had received just nine such invitations. Of the nine people who invited them in, five were strictly lonely. Three were genuinely interested in religious philosophy and the message of the church but refused to become converts. The ninth was a crazy woman who gave them doughnuts and made them watch as she held up her dog's front paws and forced him to dance on his hind legs.

One afternoon, after several more disappointments, they found themselves in a poor neighborhood, near a housing project that was in such shocking disrepair that it appeared to have been bombed and strafed. The project consisted of several two-story concrete buildings painted a dull industrial green and arranged in a semicircle on the treeless side of an adjacent hill. The windows in the buildings were broken or boarded up, and many of the doors had come unhinged and flapped in the breeze. Cars without tires, without seats or mirrors, or even engines, were parked here and there along the pitted streets.

"Looks like they had a war or something," Davis said.

Edmunds checked his map. He wanted Silbert Terrace. It was just ahead, in the middle of the project. "Quit worrying so much," he told Davis. "Who's going to listen to you if you act scared?"

Out of the buildings came juky music, booming from

portable stereo radios—expensive radios, which seemed incongruous amid the general ruin. "They must steal 'em," Edmunds whispered, when he saw a slender man in a leather jacket emerge from an apartment carrying a booming box by its handle. The man's apartment had no door at all, just a thin pink bedspread nailed into the frame. He glared at Edmunds and muttered something under his breath—some kind of curse. Edmunds ignored him, but the words seemed to float into Davis and upset his balance. He tripped over a clump of weeds sprouting through a sidewalk crack and fell down.

"Why don't you look where you're going?" Edmunds hissed.

"The faces," Davis said, rubbing his knee. "It's like my dream again."

"I don't want to hear about any dream, Walter. I swear, sometimes I think you mess up on purpose."

They walked on. Some little boys in tattered sweatshirts were tossing a football around. "Hey you!" the boys shouted. "Hey you misters, where'd you get those suits?" Edmunds waved and kept walking, being patient. Then he felt the football strike him in the small of the back. He bent to pick it up. It was made of rubber, not pigskin. He worked his fingers into the fake stitches and called to the boys. "You go on out for a pass," he said. When they didn't move, he fanned the ball back and forth with his arm. "C'mon," he yelled. "Go on out." The boys ran off in a pack, and Edmunds threw them a perfect spiral, which drifted gracefully to earth. He was pleased with himself. "That was a victory," he said.

They came at last to Silbert Terrace. It was not a bad block by project standards. It had a tufted recreation area, where children were playing on swings and slides. None of the apartments had buzzers or bells, so Edmunds and Davis had to knock when they found a door; if the door was missing, they whistled. The reception they got surprised them. Almost everybody suspected that they were from the welfare department or some other government agency, and they had to show their Utah driver's licenses before people would believe that they didn't want to cause trouble.

"Trouble is what we're here to help with," Davis said to a middle-aged man whose T-shirt had ridden up his belly.

The man accepted the leaflet. "I don't have no money to give."

"It's free. You take it now."

For a few seconds, it seemed that the man might invite them in, but he hesitated on the brink, and then said, "Well, yessir, thank you," and vanished into the gloom.

At the very next apartment, their luck changed. The man who answered their knock had splotched red eyes and a loose handshake. His skin was yellowish. A slip of paper taped to his door informed them that he was Lester Owens.

"I'd be glad for some company," he said, drawing them into a dark, musty studio apartment that smelled of cooking grease. A couple of suitcases filled with dirty clothes rested at the base of a huge color-TV console. The TV was tuned to a game show. Owens adjusted the volume, then sat on a rickety, vinyl-covered couch and put on a pair of sunglasses.

"You're getting a good picture," Davis said nervously, making conversation.

Owens smiled a little. "I'm on the cable." He sipped some colorless liquid from a teacup.

Edmunds was eager to begin. He looked around for a chair, but the couch was the only piece of furniture in the room, so he joined Owens on it. His weight, added to Owens's weight, put too much stress on the spindly legs, and the couch collapsed.

"Now you done it," Owens said, without much enthusiasm.

"I'm sorry," Edmunds said. "I didn't know it was weak."

"I'm not blamin' you, hear? It's just another thing that happened."

Davis was looking at the broken leg. "This can be glued," he said.

"Glue," said Owens, chuckling to himself. He fiddled with his sunglasses, bringing them down lower on his nose.

Edmunds slid along the collapsed couch until he was next to Owens. He showed his driver's license, and then, as calmly as he could, he told Owens about the church and its message and how it provided help in times of trouble.

"Don't you think I know about the church?" Owens asked. "Don't you think the lady was a *church* person? She sang in the choir."

"Who sang in the choir?"

"My wife did."

"Where is she now?" Davis asked.

"She's gone. She just took my baby boy and flew away."

"Flew away?"

Owens nodded. "Right into the sky," he said.

"The church we're talking about," Edmunds said, clearing his throat, "it's a different church."

"Where'd you say it's at? Utah?"

"Well, it's there, but it's here, too." Edmunds grinned and touched Owens lightly on the shoulder. "You see? Nothing can be that bad."

"I saw a TV film about Utah," Owens said. "It looked nice."

Davis set the broken couch leg on the floor by the suitcases. He studied Owens's face and tried to imagine that beneath the yellowish skin there was something he knew about—some common desire or longing. "It *is* nice," he said. "We're real close to the desert. You can ride around in your dune buggy and nobody'll bother you. The fishing's great. You should see the mountains."

"I'd like to," Owens said. "Only mountains I ever saw was on the TV. They got any work there?"

"What do you do?"

"I did construction work until they laid me off." He pointed at the TV. "Look there now. Sucker just won himself ten thousand dollars."

"They're always building new buildings in Salt Lake," Davis said.

"This church, it'd be helping me with a job?" Owens asked. "Because I could do with a church like that."

Edmunds was getting excited. It seemed to him that Owens might possibly be encouraged to attend a service. "Walter," he said, "we could talk to Mr. Harvey. He must know about thousands of jobs."

"Who's this Harvey man?" Owens scratched his cheek. "He with the unemployment?"

"Never mind," Edmunds said. He threw an arm wide,

as though he were sweeping away debris. "You don't have to live like this, Mr. Owens."

"Do tell." Owens got to his feet. "I'll be makin' some more tea now. Would you all like a cup?"

The church discouraged its members from drinking tea or coffee or any other harmful or potentially intoxicating beverage, but Edmunds thought that under the circumstances he should forget about the rule, since he'd already insulted Owens by busting his couch. "That'd be fine," he said, elbowing Davis. They followed Owens into a tiny kitchen alcove and watched him fill a dented pan with rusty tap water. He put the saucepan on a two-burner hot plate. There was a used tea bag on the counter, and Owens picked it up daintily and lowered it into the water. "Be about five minutes," he said. "Meantime, tell me more about those mountains."

Davis did his best. He described the buttes and how they turn flame-red at sunset, and described, too, the pinnacles and arches and how when you were hiking among them you felt as if you were exploring the surface of the moon. But he kept being distracted by the tea bag bobbing in the pan. Shreds of old tea were coming out of it. The idea of drinking Owens's brew was repulsive to him; he couldn't imagine what it would taste like.

"The moon," said Owens, stirring the tea. "That's where those astronauts played golf." He threw his stirring spoon into the sink, then faked a golf swing. "Bingo. Right in the eye of old Mr. Moon." This gave him the giggles, and he laughed until the water started to boil over. "Oh no, you don't!" he cried, grabbing the saucepan. He removed it from the heat, lifted out the tea bag, and poured an ounce or so of thin tea into his cup. Next, he opened a cupboard and brought down fresh cups for his guests. Obviously, they were special to him; they were china in a blue willow pattern. He filled them almost to the brim and passed them over. Edmunds crooked a finger through the handle of his cup, but Davis, who was anticipating a disgusting task, gripped his cup whole, without thinking, and promptly burned himself. The cup slipped free and dropped to the floor.

"Oh, my," said Owens, as he retrieved it. A tiny piece had chipped off the lip. He shook his head. "I know you didn't mean it."

"I didn't," Davis said earnestly. "But I'd still be glad to pay for it."

"Money can't fix something like this. This was the last good thing of hers I had, and now it's spoiled."

"Mr. Owens," said Edmunds, seeing another opportunity to take advantage of the situation. "Maybe you'd like to talk about what happened with your wife."

Owens was irritated. "I already told you, son. They laid me off. One month, two months. Repo man came around, took this, took that. So she left me. She flew away, right into the sky."

"She didn't really fly," Edmunds said, getting irritated himself.

"You don't believe it?"

"I'm sorry. I just don't. It's impossible."

"Well, I'll prove it to you." Owens yanked open a kitchen drawer and rifled through its contents, piling knives, forks, thumbtacks, and empty tape cylinders on the counter until he found what he was after. It was a photograph, a Polaroid snapshot. He gave it to Davis. "You check it out, now."

Davis was in bad shape. All the broken things were haunting him. He was suddenly afraid of Owens, of what the photo might reveal. When he looked, he saw a woman who seemed to be floating through the air. She wore a rich red robe; two gold wings sprouted from her shoulder blades.

"Is it like I said?" Owens asked. "Let me hear you."

Davis wanted to run away. "She's flying," he agreed.

This was too much for Edmunds. He snatched the photo and examined it closely. It was true that the woman appeared to be flying, but only because Owens had turned the photo sideways. When it was right side up, displayed on the vertical instead of the horizontal, it showed a choir singer who was acting a part in some religious pageant.

Edmunds was outraged. "I guess you think it's funny," he said, deliberately laying the photo on top of the wet tea bag.

"Say, listen now," Owens said. "Don't be angry. I was joking with you."

"You call that a joke?" Edmunds asked. "Somebody like you, you don't deserve our help."

"What you going to help me with?"

Edmunds was silent, but Davis, recalling his nightmare, and the ugly faces, said, "What if the world is coming to an end?"

Owens pulled his sunglasses even lower on his nose. He took a big swallow of tea. "That's old news. The world's been and gone. Why don't you let me take your picture?"

"My picture?"

"Sure. Both the two of you. I'll make it pretty. Hand me down that camera, will you?" Owens asked, pointing to a kitchen shelf. But when Davis reached for the camera, Owens stopped him. "Wait," he said. "You better let me get it. You touch it, it's bound to break." He led his subjects to the living room and positioned them near the TV. "Whether or not you smile is up to you," he said.

"Should we smile?" Davis asked Edmunds.

"Smile if you want to," Edmunds said. "I haven't decided yet."

CARAVAGGIO

W H E N I was nineteen, I won an art contest at college and used my prize of a hundred-dollar savings bond to prove to my parents that I had talent as a painter. My father, who owned a printing company, remained unconvinced, but I worked on him over the summer, becoming increasingly intolerable, and he finally agreed to support me for six months while I went to Florence to study. I left for Italy just after Labor Day, sailing from New York on a cruise ship that offered a special one-way fare to students. The morning was bright with sunshine, the Atlantic had an ultramarine color I had read about in books, and I saw myself as a hero embarking on a great adventure. I had avoided such obvious clichés as a beret or a goatee, but I carried myself with a grave self-importance, and this prevented me from making any friends my own age. Fortunately, an older couple from Detroit adopted me, and as we took our daily stroll around the deck I lectured them on Van Gogh, whose painting *Sunflowers* hung above their dining-room table, in reproduction.

We exchanged addresses in Genoa, and I caught a bus to Florence. I had enough money to rent a cheap apartment, but I didn't want to live alone, so I found a room in a pensione near the Arno River. It was booked almost solid when I arrived, but then the tourist season drew to a close, and the sisters who ran the place—Anna and Ludovica di Stefano—started behaving strangely. As soon as they had a few vacancies, they instituted a number of economy measures that seemed extreme, at least to me. They fired a chambermaid, canceled delivery of *La Nazione,* and cut back on the quality of their wine. They seldom turned on the central heating for more than an hour at a time and took to wearing shawls and heavy wool dresses. In the morning, early, I would hear them in the kitchen planning menus with Beatrice, the cook. *"Pollo,"* they said. Chicken, chicken, chicken.

Out of curiosity, I asked Anna one afternoon, in my Berlitz Italian, if the pensione had fallen on hard times. She was a formidable woman, with the muscular shoulders of a stevedore, and she merely shrugged, implying that it was none of my business. But Beatrice was more forthcoming when I put the question to her. As if she were parting with an item of gossip for which she would one day expect compensation, she told me, whispering, that the sisters were aristocrats who did not want to end badly, the way their father had done.

"But their rooms are full all summer long," I said.

"People fear what they fear," said Beatrice.

By October, the marble floor in my room was so chilly that I hated to get out of bed. Probably I would have stayed under the covers until noon if I hadn't signed up for courses at the university. Three times a week, I rode a bus across town, pressed in among strangers in overcoats and waiting for my friend Aldo to come on board. I had met him in my life-drawing class, where he managed to do superb anatomical sketches while dangling a cigarette from his lips. He was a stocky little Communist, and although he was only a year older than I, he had dark circles under his eyes and a bald spot at the back of his head. This gave him a tragic, monkish air, which he used to advantage whenever he was trying to pick up a girl or get something for nothing.

After class, we would sometimes go to a trattoria around the corner and split a liter of Chianti. In those days, I still had many fervent theories about the meaning of life, and I would lay them out shamelessly for anybody who would listen. I was in love with ideas. I would get one between my teeth and chew it until I had extracted all the juice, reducing it to its simplest terms. I wanted everything to be clear and simple. In music, I liked Bo Diddley and Wolfgang Amadeus Mozart, nothing in between. In politics, I lobbied for Jeffersonian democracy. In art, I preferred the classical, the elegant. A world of perfect definition, bathed in brilliant, hard-edged light—that was a favorite phrase of mine.

Of course, Aldo disagreed with me on almost every issue. He had his own opinions and ideas, and he accused me of being dull, unsophisticated, and poorly educated. An American.

I had never had such high intellectual conversations before, and I always got excited, drank too much wine, and invited Aldo to the pensione for some brandy. He came along reluctantly, because he knew about the di Stefano family and disapproved of them. They were part of the old order he wanted to smash. But he felt differently toward Beatrice. She was a poor young woman from the Marches, rather pretty and well built, and Aldo claimed that she aroused his partisan sympathies. I didn't believe him for an instant.

I can still remember the night he revealed his true feelings. We rolled into the pensione in our usual elevated mood, carrying on a conversation we had begun earlier. We were discussing a sensational criminal case that was featured in every tabloid. A butcher and a city councilman from Naples were feuding. For some months, the butcher had been sleeping with the councilman's wife, and when the councilman found out he systematically seduced the butcher's youngest daughter, a nubile girl who was barely into her teens. This had earned the councilman a jail term, but there was considerable public sympathy for him. I took the position that he had been wrong, regardless of the circumstances, but Aldo thought I was being naïve.

"You say that because you don't understand women," he said. "Take a look at that girl's picture sometime. Believe me, she's been around. I'll bet they know her name all over Naples." He held up a drinking glass that I had neglected to rinse out. "Please, will you ask Beatrice to bring me a clean one? If I drink from this, I could get a disease."

So I went to the kitchen and did as Aldo had asked. When Beatrice came in, she had two glasses on a tray. Aldo was sitting on my bed and thumbing through a magazine. "You look very nice tonight, Beatrice," he said. And then he added, as if the notion had just occurred to him, "You know, you don't have to work as a slave to these rich ladies."

For some reason, Beatrice thought this was hilarious.

She had to put a hand over her mouth to muffle her laughter.

"No, no, I am serious," Aldo went on. "There are other ways to earn a living. Have you ever thought about being a model at the university?"

"Model? What model?"

"In an atmosphere of creativity, there's no shame in taking off your clothes."

Beatrice dashed from the room.

"Perhaps I was too bold," Aldo said. I hit him with a pillow, and he fell over on his side and made a howling sound, like a dog crazed by the moon. "Oh, Madonna!" he cried. "She kills me with that body!"

I kept my brandy bottle in a dresser drawer. It was my ultimate weapon against the cold, so I poured it sparingly even for Aldo. The wind that seemed to blow all that winter rattled my window, and Aldo shivered and shook his head. "Really, James, why don't you move somewhere else? I thought you had bourgeois parents. Don't they send you enough cash?"

I had my excuses. The pensione was centrally located, and the food wasn't bad. If I moved, my mail would be lost. But there was actually more to it than that—only I was keeping this part a secret from Aldo, because it had me so confused.

Earlier that October, Ludovica di Stefano had stolen a shirt of mine—or borrowed it, anyway. I had hung it on a bedpost before going to sleep, but when I woke in the morning it was gone. I was upset, because I had intended to put it on again. One shirt for every three days—that was the formula I was following. I suppose I was escaping from

American standards of cleanliness; the seedy romance of Europe had me in its grip. My hair was growing longer, and I used to stand in front of mirrors and muss it around with my fingers, thinking that I looked handsome and depraved, like one of Caravaggio's young Bacchuses.

At any rate, my shirt, an old blue flannel, was missing, and when I got back from class in the afternoon I asked Beatrice if she had decided to do my laundry. She had no idea what I was talking about. But Ludovica passed by in the hall, and, overhearing us, she said, "Your shirt, James? I took it. I came into your room in the night. There was a strange noise. The wind? I am not certain. Won't you come upstairs?"

The family had its quarters on the second floor. Ludovica led me into a parlor that was furnished with antique pieces. From a mahogany armoire she brought out my shirt, plucking at it, removing threads. She had washed and ironed it, and as she placed it, neatly folded, on a chair a look of pure abstraction crossed her face. "Would you like some tea?" she asked.

While she was in her kitchen, I looked around. There were framed photos everywhere. Anna, stout and beaming in a frilly wedding dress, had an honored spot on the piano. I recognized the man by her side—Clement, her husband, who sold industrial parts. She was still married to him, after a fashion, and he lived at the pensione when he wasn't traveling to Turin or Milan. He was a dapper fellow who wore silk ties in bright colors and finely tailored Brioni suits. Even when he was around, Anna stuck to her regimen of basic black. Next to Clement's brilliance, she was as stark and charmless as a raven.

I was looking at a picture of a scrawny old man with

chins like wattles when Ludovica returned. "Our father. He was broken," she said in her faulty English.

"Dead?"

She smiled. "Yes, dead. But also broken."

This was Count Donatello di Stefano, Ludovica informed me, pulling a chair close to mine and drawing her legs up under her, so that I saw beneath her dowdy skirt a pair of thick wool stockings like those that skiers wear. Apparently, the Count had inherited tremendous wealth, but he had squandered it on such diverse things as porcelain, race horses, and mistresses. He looked so whittled away that it was hard for me to imagine him as a libertine.

"This house was just one of our houses," Ludovica said, sipping tea. "Then it became our only house. I remember the workmen bringing all the furniture up here. They were so ugly, with those big arms! When I came home from school, everything was covered with dust. Do you know who our first guest was? Harry Slade from England. I would go up to his table in the dining room and say, 'Did you visit a nice museum today, Mr. Slade?' He had no hair on his head, but he was very sweet. Anna, she thought I was terrible. 'You mustn't interrupt him,' she would say, scolding me. That was her job, because our mother was dead. But I never paid any attention. I was a forthright child. I did as I pleased."

There was a biscuit on my saucer, and I dipped it in my tea and ate it. It tasted of anise.

"I used to make up stories about the guests, too. I would tell Anna that Harry Slade had bought a leather purse on the Ponte Vecchio and had filled it with silver coins. Anna, she has a logical mind, she didn't know what to think. 'And then what, Ludovica?' she'd ask. And I would say, 'Well, Harry Slade took the coins to a woman who was hiding in an alley.' "

"I know the woman you mean," I said.

Ludovica laughed. "You must be quiet. This was a different woman anyway. A *marchesa*. And do you know what she needed the money for? She had to bribe a guard at the prison, so her husband could go free."

"What was his crime?"

"His crime? Well, I think he didn't pay his taxes." She touched her lips with a napkin. "In exchange for the coins —and there must have been a hundred of them—the woman bestowed her favors on Harry Slade."

"You tell good stories," I said.

"Now you must tell me something in return. How is your painting going? Are you enjoying our university? I once took some classes there, you know."

I had never talked intimately to an older woman, so I was a bit nervous, but Ludovica gradually put me at ease. I would guess that she was in her early thirties then. She had pale skin, dark eyes, and a slender figure. Her hair was black with a few streaks of gray, and she usually wore it in a bun, so that in profile, with her bumpy nose, she resembled fabled ladies I had seen in portraits from the Renaissance. But she wasn't beautiful by any means. If I had walked past her in the street, I wouldn't have taken notice. And yet in that parlor, with its air of history, I was drawn to her. She seemed to take me seriously; that was part of it. And I had an odd sensation, too, that she was reacting to what I said in a physical way, leaning toward me as if my words gave her sustenance.

At dusk, we heard church bells. "You must go down to

supper now," she said. "But why don't you put on your clean shirt? You shouldn't go around in that filthy sweater." When I hesitated, she said, "Go on, don't be modest."

So I slipped off my sweater. Ludovica was carrying away the tea things, and I saw her stop and glance back at me. "*Bello*," she said, with another little laugh. "Like a statue." And then she hurried off.

That afternoon marked the beginning of my confusion. Ludovica continued to do laundry for me whenever I left my clothes lying around, and although I offered to pay for the service, as other guests did, she refused my money. Instead, she asked for my company. She kept inviting me to tea, and I felt obligated to accept. At first, I didn't really want to go, but my resistance slowly vanished, and I started to look forward to our meetings. Ludovica fascinated me. When I spoke to her about art, she treated me as if I had already painted frescoes in great cathedrals. She allowed me to substitute longing for accomplishment, and I spent many hours raving at her about my dreams.

My work was going fairly well at the university, and before long I was bringing samples of it to Ludovica and seeking her approval. She had a good eye for detail. One day, I showed her a sketch of Anna I'd done on the sly, while Anna was at the front desk, bent over her ledgers and looking as monumental as Gertrude Stein in the Picasso portrait.

Ludovica studied it; she bit her lip and turned the sketch sideways. "This is your best, James," she said. "It's solid, you know? Anna, she could be a brick."

"A brick?"

"Yes, a brick. Something of value."

She had a habit of saying cryptic things like that, and I would go back to my room and review our conversations as if I had just been through a session with a Zen master. What a genius I had stumbled upon! But you have to remember that my experience with women was limited. During my freshman year in college, before my artistic yearning was in full bloom, my steady girl was a bouncy cheerleader, who made a face, pushing in her cheeks with her index fingers, if I suggested that we go to a gallery or a poetry reading instead of the Old Stone Jug.

In fact, Ludovica was so clever that I wondered why she stayed at the pensione. For Anna, the job was ideal. She had no children, her temperament was prosaic, and she enjoyed doing inventories and ordering supplies. In contrast, Ludovica took no interest in daily business affairs. She did what Anna asked her to do, but that was all. She could have been playing a game. If the pensione had sunk into the Arno, I doubt that she would have cared.

One evening when Clement was in town, I sat with him at dinner, and we got to talking about the di Stefano family. He was in a good mood, glad to be home and feeling expansive after having put away a substantial meal. "You liked the fish?" he asked me. "The sauce, it wasn't too rich?"

"No, no," I said. And then in a delicate way I broached the subject of Anna's cutbacks. Were the sisters really on the brink of poverty?

"Anna has always been a conservative person," Clement said, lowering his voice. "From the time I met her, she has been counting things. If a plate breaks, she replaces it immediately. A cup? The same. Only nineteen more left!

She has cost me sleep with her worrying, James. And then
there is the memory of her father. It still haunts her.
Donatello was a stupid man. He left his estate in a sham-
bles. Anna put it right. She was the first to ever turn a
profit here. So why shouldn't she be cautious? Besides, my
friend, this isn't the United States, where everything is
free. Gas, electricity, they cost something."

"How about Ludovica?" I asked. "She puzzles me. I
don't understand why she stays around. She's very talented,
isn't she?"

Clement grew pensive. His eyes roamed the ceiling before he spoke. "Talented, yes," he said. "But disciplined?
No. Ludovica goes through phases. A dancer, a teacher.
Then she was going to get married and have a lot of
babies. Then she started making pots, and I loaned her
money to open a ceramics shop. How long do you think
that lasted? Maybe six months before she got bored, sold
out, and moved to Rome. Meanwhile, time passes, you
see? She is a relation to me, James. Please, I don't judge
her."

My chat with Clement gave me some clues about
Ludovica's life. Since my imagination was only slightly less
fertile than hers, I was able to concoct a story about her
that satisfied me. In my version, she had gone out into the
world and suffered a trauma, probably a broken heart,
and afterward had chosen to withdraw to the pensione
rather than risk further disappointment. This fairy tale
was neat and symmetrical, but it fell apart a few days
later when I saw Ludovica leave for a night out with a
man from the neighborhood. I couldn't place him right
away; then I recalled that he sold vegetables at the central
market. How could she be dating a produce man? He was

neither heroic nor artistic, and when she went out with him again, I found to my discomfort that I was jealous.

"Your boyfriend, he seems like a decent type," I said. "Have you been going together long?"

She gave me a funny look. "We go dancing, I like to dance. Bruno dances well."

"Bruno? Is that his name?"

So the next time they went dancing Ludovica invited me along. Bruno wasn't happy about it. He wore a tight sports coat and a skinny tie, and he spoke gruffly and very fast. I could barely catch his words. "Where's your push-cart?" I wanted to say. "What do you know about grand emotions?" But I kept my mouth closed and accompanied them to a private club, in the Santa Croce district. The other club members wore skinny ties, too, along with pointy shoes, and they far outnumbered the women. From the moment we walked in, Ludovica was occupied on the dance floor. The music alternated between Beatles records and Domenico Modugno ballads, and the club, which had a low ceiling, was smoky enough to pass as a set for the Inferno. I became angry with Ludovica, because she introduced me to her friends as a young American student who was a guest at the pensione and had asked to see the real Florence. That was at odds with my sense of our relationship. I was convinced that she cared for me— deeply—and I wanted to make her admit it.

On this night, I discovered the charms of grappa. Here was a brandy that burned the stomach and lightened the brain. I drank three tumblers of it at a standup bar, feeling flames fan outward through my capillaries; and then I strolled over to Ludovica and grabbed her forearm.

"Now we are going to dance?" she asked.

"We're going to dance."

I held her at arm's length and did an old-fashioned fox-trot while a ballad played. Ludovica was very tense. The muscles in her back jumped when I touched them. As we went round the floor, she turned and waved to people, trying to distance herself from me. That made me even angrier, so I pulled her to me. "You are being foolish," she said, still twisting and turning. I held her fast, applying pressure, until she managed to break away. Everybody could see what had happened. Ludovica laughed and joked to cover her embarrassment.

Without saying anything, I left the club and wandered into a café. Somewhere in the post-midnight hours, while I was on my sodden way home, I made the mistake of hitting one of Florence's ancient palaces. I hit it with my left fist, and only the dulling effect of the brandy kept me from dropping to the ground. In the morning, I had a knuckle the size of a walnut. A doctor near the pensione gave me a splint, some bandages, and a prescription for codeine. And who should pedal by on a bicycle as I was having the prescription filled? Bruno. The Fates were clearly against me. I figured he would give me the sign of the cuckold, sticking fingers behind his head, like horns, but he just clucked his tongue in sympathy and pedaled on.

As for sympathy from Ludovica, I got none. She ignored me. You know the famous painting of Judith and the freshly severed head of Holofernes? My mind drifted toward such imagery. Obviously, I had transgressed and committed a crime of no mean proportion. In a Catholic country, the concept of perdition runs deep. Ludovica would nod to me, she would be civil, but she let it be known that she expected me to apologize.

I wasn't about to do that. I still felt angry, so for a while I stayed in my room and rested. The codeine put me in a dopey trance, and to occupy myself I did some hallucinatory sketches. Devils, pitchforks, lovers coupling in a ring of fire. I missed three meals in a row, but the only person who seemed to care was Beatrice. She brought me minestrone, pasta, and a slice of cake she must have bought at her own expense from a fancy *pasticceria*. As I ate, she sat on the edge of my bed, giving off vaporous clouds of floral perfume.

"One day, maybe two," she said. "Then you'll be better."

I showed her my purple left hand. "I'm lucky I didn't use the one I paint with."

At the mention of painting, Beatrice brightened. How did I become interested in art? What was my life-drawing class really like? How much did they pay the models?

"Why do you ask, Beatrice?"

She took a strand of dirty-blond hair between her fingers and twirled it. "Money," she said. She had a laugh that came from way down in her throat. "Why else do people do things? I have a daughter, you know. Yes, it's so. She lives with my mother in the Marches. She grows and grows. She needs money for clothes, money for her school fees. Those nuns won't let you in for nothing!"

"Your husband?" I asked.

"Ha!" She made an obscene gesture. "A coward! A real bastard, all right. I was sixteen when I married him. He had a car, a red Fiat. He was taking all the girls in our village for a ride. Do you want to hear a surprise, James?

He was no good in bed. I swear, I don't even think he liked it! One day, I joked him a bit. He had an egg every morning, soft-boiled for two minutes. So I said to him, 'Hey, Antonio! Two minutes! Just like the egg!' Maybe that was cruel, but he deserved it. And what did he do? He beat me. Look, I have a scar."

She leaned forward, pulled down the front of her dress with both hands, and presented me with an expanse of rosy skin, including significant cleavage. If she had a scar, I couldn't see it.

"Anyway, I left him after that. When a man beats you, it's time to go. Even my mother agreed. But Antonio wouldn't let me alone. He followed me around, he gave me gifts. He even went to the church and prayed for me to come back. So I had to run away." She was still holding open her dress. "Tell me honestly, now. Do you think I could be a model?"

"I think you could."

"And money? How much do they pay?" I said that I would have to ask Aldo. "That sad boy?" said Beatrice.

To Aldo I broke the news gently. "You had better not be lying," he said. He was so excited he didn't bother to ask how I'd hurt my hand. He just dragged me with him to talk with our professor, Dr. Rinaldi. This Rinaldi was a pompous man. He wore a scarf indoors and out; it was like a strange growth on his neck. Since he was always in the market for new flesh, we assumed that he paid well, but the standard rate turned out to be less than six dollars an hour. That worried Aldo. What if Beatrice refused to bare herself for such a paltry sum? So he sweetened the pot. From Rinaldi's desk he pilfered an envelope bearing the university seal, and into it he put a few bills from his wallet. I was to present the envelope to Beatrice as an advance. The balance would be due—or so I was to tell her —on the occasion of her nakedness.

Rinaldi's class was held in a tiled room that had big arched windows to deliver the light. The model posed on a wood platform, standing close to an electric space heater. The atmosphere was serious, even somber, for Rinaldi was a Leonardo scholar who believed that anatomy, its proper observation and rendering, formed the cornerstone of all great Renaissance art. If a biceps has the right quotient of blood in it, an accurate human flush, then everything else in the painting could be built upon it. You could forget about design. The body itself was a unifying principle.

Where Rinaldi had been getting his models I don't know, but I am sure they were all experienced veterans of the art school. There were more women than men, as if in aesthetic terms masculinity were inherently inferior, and they all had the look about them of athletes just over the hill. Flab and a general sagginess had set in, but they were adept at bringing forth the shape buried underneath. By judicious flexing, they performed an act of recollection and summoned the beautiful bodies of their youth, show-ing us pectorals and deltoids in astonishing relief. Circling them, Rinaldi would use a pointer to trace curves and lines, arteries and veins pumped up with blood. The models sometimes cursed when he touched them, but we never dared to laugh.

In the changing room, a faded red robe hung from a peg. A middleweight boxer might have worn it when he was no longer a contender. It fit Beatrice badly, but she was too nervous to notice. *"Permesso,"* she said as she entered. She held on to her elbows and shivered. *"Fa freddo!"* Rinaldi led her to the platform. His manner was professional and seemed to relax her. All at once, she dropped the robe, and it fell in a pool to the floor. Aldo, who was sitting next to me, unblinking at his easel, let a soft whistle escape from his lips. For a few seconds, I felt guilty about my part in the charade, but then I saw that Beatrice was losing her goosebumps. She stood straight and proud, giving her fine, full breasts a most excellent display. She turned, and smiled demurely; she was definitely a hit. Aldo pretended to be sketching her, but he could hardly hold a pencil. Desire had made him shaky and infirm. His dream had come true and had left him paralyzed.

Even after class, his hands still shook. "My cigarette," he said. "Will you light it for me?" Beatrice approached us, dressed once again, and invited herself to the trattoria. Already she had more self-confidence; she walked with more assurance. Undaunted by the fact that she had never read a book, she joined in our conversation and chopped up authors the way she chopped up onions. How difficult could intellectual talk be if Aldo and I could do it? Before going home, she told Rinaldi that she wanted regular work, and she became our steady model. Twice a week she posed for us; twice a week Aldo shelled out lire. But he paid the price willingly, because Beatrice continued to run around with us. Her daughter had a new winter coat, she told us. She was saving her own money for a fur.

Around this time we got a break in the weather—one of those rare November days when the sun tears up the clouds and sucks all the moisture from the saturated stones of the city. Instead of going to class, I helped Clement do some shopping. He was about to go on the road for six weeks and wanted to have a big holiday dinner before he left. We bought a goose and some bottles of vintage Barolo. Afterward, I was sitting on the steps of the pensione, relaxing, when I saw Ludovica walking toward me. She had been to the central market and had a net bag of vegetables slung over her shoulder. Her gait was girlish and untroubled. *"Ciao,* James," she said. "It's like springtime, no?"

I thought of the countryside. "We should take the bus to Fiesole. We could have a picnic."

"That bus is always full of people. They spoil everything. The men pinch you. The women give you the evil eye."

"It won't be that bad. Come on. Let's go."

The bus *was* very crowded. As it made its tortured way across town, it stopped at almost every corner to admit an old lady, or a schoolchild carrying books. But once we climbed into the hills the ranks began to thin, and we had space to move around. Somebody had accomplished the amazing feat of opening a window, and a warm breeze blew across my face. I smelled grass and livestock. We got off at Piazza Mino in the middle of Fiesole. A little shop was open nearby, and I bought cheese, bread, and apples. We walked from there to the Roman theater, a scallop of stone bleachers that dates from Etruscan times. I unwrapped the food and spread it on our paper bag. Blackbirds tap-danced on the seats below us.

The sun had put some color in Ludovica's cheeks. Her wool skirt was hiked up slightly. An apple and a heel of bread rested in the hammock of cloth between her knees.

"When I lived in Rome, I got to know the Romans," she said. "They think they know everything. A Roman taxi driver, he believes he's the best one in the world. No matter if he crushes his car against a building. No matter if he runs over somebody. I wouldn't go back there for anything."

"Is there any place you'd like to go?"

"Not really."

I broke up some bread and tossed pieces to the blackbirds. With their beaks they hammered the crusts. I felt loose and open, and I decided to apologize for the scene I'd made on the dance floor, but Ludovica cut me short.

"It's not your fault, James," she said. "I was the one who behaved badly. I only meant to help you by doing your laundry. Certainly I could listen to you and encourage you in your dreams. But I forgot how it is."

"How is it?"

"Well, young people are very serious. They want answers. Yes, it's true, *caro*."

There was something so final in her tone of voice that I didn't know how to respond at first. I did want answers, but what was wrong with that? Uncertainty was something I tried to avoid. I had yet to accept it as a necessary condition of being alive.

"I have missed talking to you," Ludovica said. "I think we had fun, didn't we? Before you came, I had only Anna to talk to, and Anna talks business."

"You could go out and meet people. Not everybody pinches and stares. The cafés in the city are jammed with people talking."

"They're all saying the same thing."

I threw my hands into the air.

"You don't believe me? Just wait and see, James. You'll get tired of words."

"That's just a snobbish attitude."

"So maybe I am a snob. Anyway, I'm happy enough."

"How *can* you be happy enough? You told me a minute ago you were lonely."

"Answers," she said, smiling at me. "Yes, you want them."

All this was bringing me down. I had not come to Fiesole on a sunny afternoon to listen to a lecture, so I suggested that we walk some more. It was siesta time, mid-afternoon, and as we toured the narrow, cobbled streets, moving through pockets of light into the shade, there were no sounds except from muffled radios. The entire town was dozing, and I wondered if anything was actually happening. This was a variation on the ancient "If a tree falls in the forest" routine, but it kept me occupied. Was the pumping of waking blood more significant somehow than the pumping of blood in sleep? And so on and so forth.

Ludovica walked beside me, her head down and her hands locked behind her back. I was tempted to reach out and touch her, but I did not. Instead, I started describing to her a painting I was working on. This seemed to please her, so I did some inventing, adding details that had not yet found their way to the canvas. I made the painting very grand, and by the time we came to the bus stop it had surpassed the dimensions of the Sistine Chapel. I would have painted it on the hills and on the sky if that was what it took to get the job done.

The weather reverted to type for Clement's dinner, but for once we were comfortable inside, because Anna had put on (and left on) the central heating. Not only that—

she and Ludovica wore dresses with color in them for a change. Clement contributed to the festivities by carting down an old Victrola and playing opera records for us when he wasn't in the kitchen supervising Beatrice. The goose cooked to arias from Puccini, throwing off spatters of fat. I sat on a couch and talked to a young Swiss couple from Zurich, honeymooners, who, along with a friend of Clement's, were the only other guests.

Clement was a gracious host. The goose arrived on the table, and he took carving tools to it and soon had the breast meat layered in rows. With a flick of his wrist he severed a wing, and I couldn't help thinking of Dr. Rinaldi's belief that anatomy was the key to understanding. A trickle of grease ran down my chin as I bit into a leg. Beatrice brought around a brimming gravy boat. Beneath her apron was a straight skirt; she had a date with Aldo and me later on.

Throughout the meal, Clement and his friend told bawdy jokes. Anna and Ludovica were surprisingly light-hearted. They giggled and teased each other, as they must have done when they were girls. When the dishes were cleared, Clement put away Puccini and started playing cha-cha records, and before long he was dancing a strange fandango with the Swiss girl. I looked at Ludovica and thought I would ask her to dance. I still had a notion that we had something to resolve. But then the buzzer of the pensione sounded, and up the stairs came Bruno, taking them two at a time. He looked much better to me. Maybe he'd had a bath or a haircut; I couldn't tell for certain. After he had shaken hands and kissed cheeks, he sat next to Ludovica and threw his arm around her. He could have been gathering her in; the gesture smacked of possession. It was simple, direct, and unequivocal, and I was hurt to see that she did not resist.

I would have crawled to my room and disappeared if Beatrice hadn't insisted that we meet Aldo. So I put on my coat and went out. And there was poor Aldo at our favorite café, sitting at a table with two chairs tipped up against the edge, reserved for us. Under a dull, yellow light bulb, with smoke curling around his monkish face, he looked like a man who had been thinking the same thought for a million years. He leaped to his feet when he saw us and fussed over Beatrice. Could he buy her a drink? What about a cappuccino? Overheated and lovelorn, he exposed himself to her indifference.

"I have been reading in Schopenhauer," he announced, and Beatrice closed her eyes and pretended to snore. She'd had enough of talk; she wanted to play the pinball machine. It was an old one, manufactured by Chicago Coin. It had pictures of gangsters on the display panel and made a siren noise if you hit a cop's shield with a ball. Beatrice really loved it. She was louder than the siren. She shrieked when she used the flippers, and she was not above addressing the balls as if they had free will and could be coerced into obeying orders. "Go in that hole, *cretino!*" she'd shout. A ball's failure to comply provoked her. She would slip off a high-heeled shoe and tap the glass. "Pay attention, you!"

We closed the café that night. Aldo stood outside the locked door, waving to us, with the collar of his trenchcoat turned up. A waiter was sweeping the floors inside, spreading sawdust over dead cigarettes. On the way home, Beatrice took my arm. She had scored a record number of points, and she sang, in her gravelly voice, some words from a pop tune: *"Sapore di sale, sapore di mare."* A taste of salt, a taste of the sea. I became aware of her perfume, which had seemed so overpowering to me before. "You smell good," I said. And I pushed my face into her hair.

The pensione was quiet. Together we walked down the hall, and Beatrice came into my room. "You're not allowed in here," I said, teasing, and she laughed and threw her coat on the bed. The heat was still on, and for once the room felt warm and accepting.

"I am going to pose for you, James," Beatrice said. "Wouldn't you like that?" All I could do was smile. She took off her sweater and skirt and stood before me in a red silk teddy that she must have worn for Antonio on their wedding night. Down came her stockings, slowly; and then she removed her lingerie. With no academic distance to separate us, I was forced to revise my opinion of her. I did so by entering a state the mystics describe as "bliss." I had a moment's guilt, thinking about Aldo, but when Beatrice joined me in bed she deprived him of his existence. Oh, the miraculous rewards of a life of confusion!

When I woke in the morning, Beatrice was still beside me. I could hardly believe my good luck. I thought I should bring her some coffee, so I put on my pants and went to the kitchen. There I found Bruno, barefooted, wearing what must have been an old robe of Ludovica's. He had a tray before him, and on it were two cups, two hard rolls, and a jar of marmalade. He was staring at the tray, moving things around. He would put the cups on one side, then on the other. The marmalade stayed in the middle, blazing like the sun.

TOO MUCH
ELECTRICITY

G O R D Y got into the moving business by accident, when he was hitching down to L.A. from Oregon after a long summer of ranch work. Eighty-four cars passed him by outside Portland before a small truck with Idaho plates pulled over. Some lightweight chairs were strapped to the cab. The driver offered Gordy a smoke from a crushed pack of Camels and then said in an offhand way, staring at Gordy's muscular chest, "Looks like you been pumping a lot of iron."

Well now, Gordy thought. He folded his arms and touched his biceps protectively, fearing the onset of highway weirdness. "It comes from digging postholes," he said. He slid toward the door and watched the macadam slipstreaming by. Could he jump if things got bad? Not without dying. So he said to the driver, "I think you ought to know I have a Buck knife strapped to my ankle. It's sharp enough to shred onions."

"Wait a minute," the driver said. "This is some kind of misunderstanding. I got a job of moving to do. My buddy, he was supposed to ride down with me, but he got drunk last night and flaked out. If you help me unload the truck when we get to Los Angeles, I'll pay you seventy dollars flat."

Gordy considered the proposition. The cash sounded attractive. "I'll do it if you pay me in advance," he said.

"Half before and half after. They only paid me a deposit so far."

"Deal," Gordy said, shaking hands.

The driver's name was Earl Phillips. He told Gordy he did these long hauls only once in a blue moon. People traveling from state to state usually hired a brand-name mover, because brand-name movers were responsible and professional and all that crap. "It's just advertising," he said. "Those old boys bang stuff around like the rest of us do."

"You ever move a piano?" Gordy asked.

"Not too many pianos in Boise," Phillips said.

They reached L.A. the next day and drove out toward the ocean through traffic and neon streaks. Gordy hadn't seen the city for six months. He felt tired and dreamy, relaxed in every particular, and he started singing softly to himself, barely opening his mouth. The song was one he'd written in Oregon. It wasn't country-and-Western, but it had some mountains in it. It had trees and a river. It was clear.

"You have a nice voice," Phillips told him. "Not too high and not too low."

"Before I dropped out of college, I used to play the club scene around here. I was in a band for a couple of years."

"Sure you were."

"Hey, I'll prove it to you." Gordy leaned toward Phillips

and bowed his head, so that it was directly in Phillips's line of vision. "Check out my hair."

Phillips turned on the dome lights and ran his fingers over Gordy's scalp. "I'll be damned," he said. "There's a little bit of purple in it."

"It used to be all purple. But I had a fit and cut it off with a pair of nail clippers."

"Nail clippers!" Phillips shrieked. "I never heard of such a thing."

Gordy laughed. "Now you know why I needed a vacation," he said.

The barbering incident had taken place after a very dissatisfying gig at a Hollywood club where the audience started beating each other up with broken-off chair legs even before the band finished its first number. Gordy was furious about the stupidity of it all. In his apartment, aided by a fifth of Rémy Martin, he reduced his skull to brown and purple nubbins; then he packed a knapsack and headed for the airport. A friend from his abortive college days managed a cattle ranch east of Portland, and Gordy had stayed with him once before when his circuits had got fried. This time, the friend put him in a bunkhouse with two local guys, who taught him to spit between his teeth and carve figurines from deadfall. They were impressed that he'd cut a record with his band, and they wanted the inside scoop on the music business. "First off, it doesn't have anything to do with music," Gordy said.

Before long, he was helping his bunkmates with their daily chores. Out on the range, he mended fences and rode herd on strays. Muscles he hadn't used since grade school suddenly doubled in size, and he had to buy a new supply of T-shirts at a country store that had a rack full of the latest paperback romance novels. Gordy read *Love's End-less Ache*. He read *Pomegranate Autumn* and *Nurse Reilly's Affair*. Then, in the midst of all those passionately beating hearts, he found something called *Secrets of the Ancients*, which was about the great religions of the world, and he read it through in a sitting, learning important lessons about meditation, karma, and the path to peace and understanding. When his former manager finally stopped phoning he interpreted it to mean that his previous incarnation as a purple-haired keyboard man for Vampire Baby had officially been terminated. He took a certain pleasure from the loss of that life. Eight to go, he told himself.

One afternoon, while he was pitchforking hay, he heard some music in his head and paused to scribble a couple of lines in a pocket notebook. He took this as a sign of health. It reminded him of experiences he'd had before he'd joined the band, back when he was struggling to write honest songs. The music continued day after day, and he decided he was ready to return to the city. His friend tried to discourage him, but Gordy wouldn't listen. "Don't worry about me," he said. "I know I can break the cycle." It was a matter of pride to him, putting things right in a context of chaos.

The address Earl Phillips was looking for was in Santa Monica. He got lost twice before he found the right little stucco bungalow. It belonged to a writer who'd just sold his first screenplay to Twentieth Century-Fox. The sale had allowed him to give up his teaching position at the University of Idaho, divorce his wife, and move to California with a former student. It was the student who explained all this to Gordy as he was carrying in boxes of books. She was young, blond, and built for speed. She said that Robert De Niro might be interested in starring in the movie—at least, some agent who knew his agent thought he might be interested—and that several directors, including Steven Spielberg and George Lucas, had asked to see the script.

"Life will be very different for me here," she said. "Idaho was so, I don't know—boring."

Another lost one, Gordy thought. "Excuse me, please, miss," he said. "I need to put these where you're standing."

Gordy liked the moving work. It was simple and direct and left his mind free to wander. When it came time to bring in the heavy stuff, Phillips showed him a different grip to use. The writer's couch—a flagrant black leather item—put a crimp in his back. "Just let it down real easy," Phillips advised him. "It's only got those skinny little legs." Next, they strapped a washer to their dolly and wheeled it in. The truck was empty now, except for some paintings wrapped in old blankets. Gordy peeked at one. It was squiggly red lines on soiled canvas, with no discernible shape or pattern. Too much electricity, he thought.

Sweat ran down Phillips's cheeks and nose as he latched the truck door. He gave Gordy a fifty-dollar bill. "That makes eighty-five all told," he said. "The bonus is because you're a good worker. How'd you like to buy me supper?"

They had steak sandwiches and chocolate malts at a diner on Wilshire Boulevard. Gordy watched the cook slaving over a flaming grill. "I worked in a hash house when I first came down here to go to U.C.L.A.," he said. "The grease smell gets into your skin. You become a walking hamburger."

"What were you studying?"

"Music theory and composition. I wanted to be a song-writer. But then I started messing around with a synthe-sizer. Next thing I knew I was onstage in some joint on the Strip, biting the neck of a mannequin."

Phillips chewed thoughtfully on a French fry. "You going to join up with your band again?" he asked.

"You make me sound like Jesse James, man."

"I'm just a country boy, Gordy. I don't always say things right."

"What I'll probably do is drive a cab," Gordy said. "I've done that before, too. When I get enough money together, I may go into the studio on my own."

"You ought to look into the moving business," Phillips said, signaling for the check. "It's independent work. You can buy a truck pretty cheap. The first few months might be tough until you establish a reputation, but after that it'd be smooth."

"Can you really make a living at it?"

"You know what a bass boat is?"

Gordy nodded. "The kind with chairs. Built for bass fishing."

"I own one of those outright," Phillips said.

In Laurel Canyon, Gordy found a tiny one-room cottage to rent. Although the place was trashed, the landlady in-sisted that he pay a cleaning deposit, and he had to fork over seven hundred dollars in all. The outlay almost ex-hausted the bankroll he'd earned in Oregon. What little he had left went toward a down payment on an old Ford truck that had been involved in an accident on the

Ventura Freeway. He bought it from the Count of Discount, who specialized in Vehicular Mayhem, with particular attention to the Slashing of Automotive Prices.
"I'm not going to lie to you, son," the Count said, tugging
on his goatee. "This vehicle needs brakes. It might could
use a clutch. The transmission's not so hot. But where else
are you going to get just what you want at a price you
can afford?"

Gordy put the truck up on blocks in the driveway of
the cottage, slid beneath it, and studied its innards. The
Count had indeed not lied to him. Copious oil and motor
sludge dripped onto his head. He spent the next week
scavenging appropriate parts from junkyards. When he
had the truck running, he painted the outside a deep
metallic blue. Then, in flowing yellow script, he wrote on
it *A Moving Experience.* But that night he slept poorly,
troubled by the notion that he was being cute; he could
feel his lips on the neck of the cold plastic mannequin
again. So in the morning he painted over the script and
changed it to substantial white block letters that read
GORDON SLAUGHTER MOVING, INC.

As Earl Phillips had warned him, business was slow at
first. There was a lot of competition for the marginal work
of moving singles and young marrieds from one apartment
to the next. Gordy put ads in two shopper newspapers and
in an artsy New Wave sheet, but almost a month went by
before anyone phoned him about a job. His first call was
from an airline stewardess who said she'd had it with
Marina del Rey; she was going to Venice, where the people
were more in tune with her life style. Gordy sucked in his
breath and asked her, in his best professional manner, to

inventory her possessions. They struck a bargain, and Gordy went out to hire an assistant mover. It wasn't difficult for him to get help—in Los Angeles struggling musicians outnumber successful ones by about ten thousand to one.

Gordy hooked up with Ollie Squeeze, a big Jamaican who was knocking around town trying to cut it as a reggae man. Ollie had a twice-a-week gig at a punk club in Encino, but it didn't pay much, and he was glad for the extra money. On moving day, Ollie showed up at the cottage in bright-orange coveralls. He had a Dodgers cap on top of his dreadlocks. "I been doin' roadie work, mon," he told Gordy as they drove over to the stew's place. "Totin' around amplification for some New Jersey boys. Heavy metal! It do affect me in the negative. Now furniture totin becomes my line of work. I tell you true, Gordon, there ain't no justice here in Babylon."

Ollie was strong and eager, but he had a tendency to wrestle with every object as though it were a demon, and Gordy had to instruct him in delicacy. Still, they finished the job in a very short time. The stewardess was happy to arrive at her new condominium with all her glassware intact, so she referred two of her friends to Gordy, after which he got a pilot and a woman who worked for a rental-car agency. In a little while, he had enough jobs to pay the rent on his cottage and provide some upkeep for the truck. He banked everything extra in an interest-bearing checking account, thinking that he'd use it someday to cut a solo album, or at least a 45. He wanted to pay for it himself, so there'd be no interference from record companies or managers or anybody else who might meddle with the material. The music would be simple, pure, directly from the heart.

One afternoon, Gordy and Ollie went to Redondo Beach to move a Valerie, no last name given. The woman who answered Gordy's knock was so hideously deformed that he had to look away. She had great wens and blisters all over her face. After motioning for Ollie to stay in the truck, Gordy followed her inside and got another shock when she touched her cheek and peeled off a hunk of skin. It took him a moment to realize that the skin was latex— some kind of mask. He watched in silence as she continued her peeling, dropping fragments of fake skin on the apartment floor.

"I almost didn't get here in time," she said as she walked toward the kitchen, where hot water was steaming in the sink. "The damn director kept shooting my scene over and over again. I mean, really, how artistic can a shot of corpses be?" She peeled off the last of her mask, then began bathing her face. "I swear, I feel like I've been in the grave for forty years." Her real skin was shiny and unflawed. "It's like I'm trapped in a cliché."

"I know you from somewhere," Gordy said, trying to place her.

"Did you ever work as an extra out at the studio?"

It came to him then. "You were living in Santa Monica with that writer. You were my first moving job."

She looked at him in recognition. "You have a lot more hair," she said.

"This is really amazing," Gordy said. *Secrets of the Ancients* had spoken about the importance of people who turn up unexpectedly. "It must be my karma to meet you again." He remembered the screenwriter's couch, and said, "I guess things didn't work out for you over there."

"Charlie's nuts," she said flatly. "His deal fell apart, and he started doing coke. He kicked me out. I didn't have a cent, so I called some of his friends and one guy set me up with this extra's job in a grave-robbing flick."

"So you're moving downtown?"

She nodded. "There's this residential hotel somebody told me about. It's not too bad. No roaches, anyway. At least, it's cheaper than this place."

Gordy waved to Ollie, and they loaded the truck. There wasn't much to carry—a secondhand armchair, a mattress, a box of clothing, a hot plate, some kitchen things. The hotel was a decaying structure without any air conditioning. It had no roaches, but it housed many other varieties of insect life. Valerie paid Gordy in ones and fives, carefully pulling each bill from a child-sized coin purse. He watched her turn and climb the stairs, thinking how foolish she'd been to fall into such an obvious trap. "There's one who never should have left Idaho," he said to Ollie, shaking his head.

But that night, when he couldn't get her out of his mind, he saw the situation differently. Hadn't he made the same kind of mistake when he'd dropped out of school to join the band? You couldn't blame people for being susceptible to dreams. A sympathetic impulse began to gnaw at him. He worried about Valerie all the next day—the hotel was full of junkies and perverts—and in the evening, after he'd showered, he drove back over there and went up to her room. She was sitting in her armchair, eating Japanese soup noodles from a coffee cup and watching the news on TV.

"Now, don't take this the wrong way," Gordy said, being as clear about things as he could be. "I'm not trying to hit on you." He told her that if she wanted to she could move in with him until she got her life into gear. His cottage wasn't much, but he kept it neat and it had no bugs other than the common ones. "Bugs you'll know and love," he said. "Ants, flies, maybe a spider."

She laughed and offered him a spoonful of soup. He slurped it and then carried her stuff to the truck. He slept in there that night, on her ratty old mattress, with the truck door open, while she made herself comfortable in his bed.

Three days later, when it rained, he joined her in the bed, although they didn't become lovers right away. He tried touching her, but she stopped him and turned on her side. "I have a bad history with men," she said.

Gordy used his knuckles to rub her back. "It's okay," he said. "We don't have to do anything." Pretty soon, he fell asleep, taking surprising comfort from the simple fact of a warm body next to his. Valerie had a funny way of breathing. It reminded him of the sound young heifers on the ranch had sometimes made. "Deviated septum," she told him when she woke. "It's my birth defect."

She walked naked to the shower and walked out of it naked and slipped casually into her underwear. This was only the first example of her gift for intimacy. She liked secrets and gossip, and there seemed to be nothing she wouldn't confide to him. In less than a week, Gordy learned that her breasts were of a remarkably even shape and size, that she used a rinse on her hair, and that she hated to shave under her arms. She also gave him a great deal of information about her family, so that he became an expert on the Hawthornes of Idaho, their many branches and offshoots. He'd figured from the start that she'd run off with Charlie the writer simply to escape, but she confirmed it for him anyway, and told him that Charlie had been her eighteenth lover. She was twenty-two years old.

Gordy kept his mouth closed about his own past. He liked the idea that Valerie might have fallen for a furniture mover. In his Vampire Baby days, it had bothered him sometimes to think that the women he went with were interested only in his status as a semi-star, but he had to admit that there were other times when he hadn't cared at all. Anyway, the thing with Valerie was a novelty to him— sweet and innocent, a part of his new life; he was willing to let it be. He stored his music notebooks in a drawer, and Ollie, who was sworn to secrecy, arranged for him to practice piano at a friend's rehearsal hall once a week.

Valerie was eager to explore the city with him; eager for discos and clubs and L.A. flash. She wanted to visit all the spots that Charlie—being too old—wouldn't take her to. Gordy begged off, claiming to be low on funds, but there wasn't much he could do when, after her final day as an extra, she insisted on blowing her paycheck on a little action. "Let's do something wild," she said. "Let's go to the Brown Derby. I want to eat inside a hat."

From his closet Gordy unearthed a suit coat and a thin pink tie. Valerie wore a vagrantly flowing dress of powder blue, with her hair piled high, prom-queen style. They drove in the moving truck and parked a block away. The maître d' didn't like the look of them and gave them a table near the kitchen. "Don't you love Hollywood?" Valerie asked Gordy, sipping on an Orange Blossom.

She kissed him in the truck afterward and started breathing funny, and said that if she made it with him he shouldn't interpret it as a commitment or anything like that. She was very serious but also very hot.

Gordy's own breath did something odd. "Fine," he said, and returned her kiss.

Valerie remained very hot. After a month or so of intense adventure, Gordy began to wonder if she was trying to compensate for being out of work. There was nothing else for her at the studio, especially without Charlie's juice, or the juice of his friends, and she frequently complained of being useless and leeching off other people. She had no idea what she wanted to do with herself. She perked up when he took her to an occasional movie, but the rest of the time she was a pain. "For all the fun we have," she complained, "I might as well be back in Idaho."

Gordy tried to be gentle with her. "Something will come along if you're patient," he said.

"But I'm bored right now, Gordy." She gave him a coquettish look. "Why can't I help you and Ollie on the truck?"

"Don't be silly," Gordy said.

But Valerie persisted. Women climbed telephone poles and fixed the wires; they went down into the mines of Kentucky; they were cops and firefighters.

"All right," Gordy said, getting up from his armchair. It was a heavy old Art Deco item he'd bought at a thrift shop, and, as a test, he asked her to move it across the room. She rolled up her sleeves and pushed it. There were bad scratches on the floor when she was done, and he pointed them out to her.

"You're the same as Charlie," Valerie said. "You treat women like dirt."

So Gordy put her on the truck. He let her carry boxes, lamps, paintings—all the easy stuff. She was more in the way than anything else, but he ignored it, since he was certain that she'd tire of the work before long. Her arms hurt, her legs hurt, she had blisters on her feet. At night, he ran hot baths for her and afterward rubbed her down with baby oil, touching his lips to her slippery skin. She was crazy but alluring. He was beginning to love her a little bit.

There was a night when everything seemed perfect. He sat down at their rickety table and ate a dinner of stir-fried vegetables she'd cooked. She was wearing a robe, and her hair was wet at the tips from her bath. He recognized again that she was beautiful, but that wasn't what appealed to him then. It was more the rightness of her, in the small kitchen, eating the brilliantly colored vegetables with her chopsticks. You are full of romantic crap, he told himself, looking away, but the idea of rightness, or perfection, stayed with him later, when he sat outside and breathed the terrible canyon air and listened to the traffic on the perilous roads below him. The night was really big and sweeping. He wanted to fix the moment in his mind, knowing even as he tried that he was probably putting too much stress on something that wasn't meant to take it.

In Playa del Rey, the very next morning, against his better judgment he let Valerie help him move a heavy mahogany armoire. She dropped her end, and he sprained

his back so badly that he had to go to a doctor. The prescription was for muscle relaxants and bed rest. The pills
kept him in such a goofy stupor that he had to cancel a
job. He thought he'd be fine in a day or two, but even after
resting he was still so stiff and sore he could barely walk.
Valerie had to help him into his clothes. He made it to the
truck and climbed into the cab, but when he stretched a
leg toward the gas pedal he pinched a nerve along his spine
and howled in pain.

"You're not doing what the doctor told you to do,"
Valerie said.

"If I stay in bed much longer, I'll be out of business."

"Ollie and I can handle things."

Gordy wouldn't accept this; he argued with her about
her inexperience. "Okay, okay," she said. But once she had
him bedded down again, she lifted the keys from his pants
and went out and did a job. He could see how proud she
was when she came home, so he didn't say anything about
the smell of burning rubber or the horrible whine the
transmission made as she wheeled the truck up the hill.

Valerie did another job that week, and one the next,
while Gordy stayed in bed and smoldered. His back wasn't
getting any better, so he went to the hospital for some
X-rays. The pictures showed that he was developing a disc
problem. A young intern examined him, manipulating his
spine with icy fingers, and mentioned the possibility of
corrective surgery. "Fat chance I'd let you cut me, man!"
Gordy cried. Immediately he was sorry and apologized for
having lost his temper. All during the bus ride home, he
did silent meditation, but the sight of the cottage strewn
with Valerie's dirty clothes—she didn't have time for the

laundry anymore—upset him again. He decided to tape his X-rays to the wall, so she could see with her own eyes the damage she'd done.

He made some soup for dinner, thinking she'd be there to share it with him, but she was late getting home. When she hadn't arrived by ten o'clock, Gordy just assumed that she'd cracked up the truck out in Encino, where she'd gone to move some newlyweds into a tract house. Probably it was the truck's karma, he thought. It would keep having accidents, over and over again, until its truck soul soared off to Nirvana, or whatever that Indian holy place was.

He was dozing when Valerie finally came in. "How bad?" he asked sleepily.

"What do you mean, 'How bad?' " she asked.

"I mean how bad was the goddamn wreck?" He switched on the light and saw that she was giggling. She was wearing Ollie's cap backward, like a catcher.

"The only thing that's wrecked is me," she said.

Valerie had a story to tell. After they finished with the newlyweds, Ollie asked her if she wanted to stop in for a drink at the club where he played. So they stopped. The club was dark, smoky, with Mylar on the walls. The bartender wore a vest made of beer-can poptops over his bare chest. Valerie would have been ill at ease if Ollie hadn't known everybody. He introduced her to a bunch of punks at the bar. At first, she thought they were too aggressively disgusting to be believed, but once she'd talked to them for a while she began to enjoy herself. She felt obligated to buy a second round, since Ollie had bought the first, and she almost got into a fight with the bartender when she asked him to make her an Orange Blossom. He said it was an upscale drink and gave her a beer and a shot of mescal instead. "Unreal," she said when she saw a worm inside the mescal bottle. She'd always thought that such worms belonged to the realm of special effects. When she told this to the bartender, he rattled his vest, poured the mescal into a wine carafe, and fished out the worm with a long-handled spoon. "Eat it," he said, and Valerie, feeling herself on the spot, opened her mouth and somehow managed to get it down.

"It had like a magical effect," she said, kneeling next to Gordy on the bed, with her eyes wide. "All I wanted to do was dance."

"You should have had the decency to let me know where you were," Gordy told her. "I've been lying here worrying about you."

"Don't play daddy. I'm a big girl." She touched his cheek. "Poor Gordy. When you get better, we'll go out there together and dance."

"No way."

"Never say never, Gordy. Besides, it would do you good to cut loose once in a while." She glanced around the room and made a face. "What's that junk on the walls?"

"X-rays," Gordy said.

Almost a month passed before Gordy, wearing a back brace, was ready to work again. By then, Valerie had got her hair cut in a geometric style that was longer on one side than on the other. In her right ear she wore a pendant earring in the shape of a golf club. She had her own Dodgers cap to match Ollie's.

Two or three nights a week, she went out to the club and stayed until three or four in the morning. For a while, she tried to drag Gordy along, but then gave up. "People can be together without having all the same interests, right?" she asked. And Gordy said, "Sure they can," although he was becoming increasingly intolerant of her infatuation with the scene. He tried to control his temper, but he found himself picking at her silly clothes and accusing her of having a bad attitude.

"Just lay off me," she said, pacing around the cottage. "You know what you are? You're like a Fascist. You're so superior, you want everybody to be just like you."

"That's not it," he said. "C'mon, Valerie, you're not sixteen anymore. You ought to act your age."

"What do you want me to do? You want me to settle down and have ten kids and feed them Mrs. Paul's Fish Sticks and all that crap? I don't have to be on TV, Gordy. It's almost the twenty-first century. Why shouldn't I enjoy myself before I get old?"

Then one night she didn't come home at all. Gordy tossed and turned and thought about calling the cops to report her absence, but he knew in his heart that nothing was wrong.

He was looking out the window the next morning, brushing his teeth, when he saw her get out of a rusty Datsun. The driver he knew from the old days—green-haired, snaggle-toothed, the guy played rhythm guitar for Instant Despair.

"Don't tell me," he said when she walked in. "You're just friends."

"As a matter of fact, we are," Valerie said. "All we did was buy a bottle of wine and go out to the beach for the sunrise."

"Ain't love grand?" Gordy said.

Somehow he expected the indiscretion to make her

guilty, but after work she put on her makeup and her new leopard-skin pants and left without a word. She strolled downhill from the cottage, wobbling a little on her stiletto heels; then she picked up the pace and ducked around the corner, to where the Datsun was idling. He watched her get in and lean toward the driver and kiss him on the cheek.

For more than an hour, Gordy sat on his bed with his legs crossed and let positive images flow through his mind. He thought of pastureland rippling under a noon sun, of rain drumming on the bunkhouse roof. He decided to cool out by practicing some piano, but on the drive to the rehearsal hall he went by a twenty-four-hour dime store and wandered in. Everywhere ugly people were buying ugly merchandise they didn't need. Gordy had a sudden desire for a personalized black sweatshirt bearing the motto *Niceness Is Down for the Count,* but some wimp clerk behind the counter refused to print it, on the ground that it didn't make sense. Gordy couldn't believe it. "You know what doesn't make sense?" he yelled. "The way people live their lives!" In the toy department, he found a miniature electric organ, and he began fingering the keys. When he couldn't get any volume out of the goddam thing, he put it on the floor and jumped on it.

By the time he got to the club where Valerie hung out, he'd lost all control. A couple of customers at the bar recognized him as a former headliner and bought him drinks. Instant Despair was due to take the stage at midnight, after the warmup band finished its set, and Gordy asked the club manager if he could go backstage to the greenroom and pay his respects. Valerie was there, sitting on an old couch. The guitarist was next to her, with his arm around her shoulders. "Hey, wow, Gordy man, have a beer," he said.

"You *know* him?" Valerie asked.

"Sure, Val. He was with Vampire Baby. A very hot band from the past. What, like 1985, Gordy?"

Gordy removed the guitarist's sunglasses and looked him in the eye. "This is a great country," he said. "I don't want to hear any bad words about it in any of your songs. You got that?"

"Sure," the guitarist said. "I hear you on that. Have a beer, man."

Gordy accepted the beer and drank it in a swallow. He shook hands politely with the guitarist. Then he grabbed the guy's rhythm guitar and smashed it to bits. He hitched up his jeans and said to Valerie, "Don't you dare think that had anything to do with love."

"How could I love somebody who lied to me?" Valerie said. Clearly, she was hurt. "You didn't trust me. You were playing games."

"I wasn't playing games."

"You lied to me," Valerie said. "I knew you were as bad as Charlie."

Gordy couldn't stand the confusion. He couldn't remember anymore what he'd intended to say to her, or even what he'd hoped for. "Well, I wasn't playing games," he said, but she wouldn't look at him. She had her hand on the shoulder of the guitarist, who was mumbling threats while he sifted through the splinters and busted strings. Gordy said, "Okay, see you later. I'm going outside to wreck the truck."

"You what?"

"Going outside to wreck the truck."

The truck was in the parking lot. Gordy climbed into the cab, feeling both stupid and liberated. He laughed to himself, started the engine, and backed up to a point some ten yards from a concrete pillar. Then he strapped himself in and drove directly into the pillar at a speed designed to maximize damage while still preserving the driver's health. Impact was forceful and loud. The hood buckled. The radiator was demolished, along with part of the engine block. Gordy bumped his nose lightly on the dashboard. Through hissing steam and a shower of spray, he saw Valerie standing in the doorway of the club, looking so ashen that she seemed already to have become a ghost from some forgotten time.

Ollie Squeeze drove Gordy home in a borrowed car. Whenever Gordy's head flopped forward, Ollie would push it back with the palm of his hand and say wearily, "Provocation of the complication, Gordon. Provocation simple and true."

Gordy slept through the night and into the next afternoon. He didn't really expect Valerie to be there when he woke, but he still felt a slight pang of loss to find that she hadn't returned. He thought of her in bed with him and shivered. The very dimensions of the cottage appeared to have changed. After many cups of coffee, he wrote a note and left it for her, knowing she'd be back sooner or later for her clothes. He told her that he owed her some money for her work, but that he didn't have much of it— the best he could do was a check for five hundred dollars, which was all he had in his interest-bearing account. She could also have the truck if she wanted to bother with the repairs. He apologized for what he'd done, and said that he was planning to leave town. He had this friend in Oregon he stayed with whenever things got heavy, and they were heavy now. He propped the note against an empty beer can and put a few belongings into his knapsack. On his way out of the cottage, he promised himself that he would do better next trip, and that if he didn't do better he would continue to repeat the trip until he got it right.

GIORGIO'S MOTHER

ON SABBATICAL in Rome, Thomas Burnham, who taught art history at an Ohio junior college, developed a knot in his lower back from hunching over documents in museums and libraries. Swimming was the only thing that had ever helped him with such pains, so he consulted a phonebook and located a club with a pool, not far from his apartment. *Amici dell' Aqua*, it was called—Friends of the Water. Burnham was amused by the name, thinking that there must be something peculiarly Italian about claiming to be friendly with one of the elements. It suggested a casual approach to body maintenance, even a belief in universal harmony. Copying the address on a scrap of paper, he set off for the club on a brilliant spring afternoon. The city was shades of rose and umber, and the Tiber was running clear.

At the gate, Burnham encountered an unexpected problem. A stout dwarf of a woman was on guard duty, and she was as inflexible in her attitude as a figure carved into a frieze. She refused to understand anything he said until, in frustration, he identified himself as a *professore*. No further details were required of him after that. To the guard, a title of any kind meant class, breeding, and, most important, wealth. Grinning now, her round face beaming as if she'd won a lottery prize, she led him to an office near the pool and went to arrange an audience with the direttore, who, judging by her respectful tone, was only slightly less sanctified than the Pope.

Burnham waited on a couch. Through an open window, he watched light fall on crumbling buildings and felt loneliness well up in him. He missed his daughters, his students, and his familiar routine at home. For a moment he became so melancholy that he had to remind himself how much he'd looked forward to this period of isolation. On an earlier sabbatical, in Tuscany, he had written a monograph on the significance of madonnas in the secular life of the Renaissance, and he had hoped to expand it and advance his career. But in all his digging through the stacks, he had yet to find anything really sensational, and out of disappointment, he'd been consoling himself with pasta, bread, and gelato, adding twelve pounds to his frame.

The direttore was a tall, robust fellow whose clothes smelled strongly of tobacco. His English, though plentiful, was not good, but still he offered it as a gift. From his desk he produced an elaborate application blank, and when Burnham had completed it, he shook his head sadly and said that the club was not accepting new members. Already, the pool was too crowded during lap swim. Men were colliding with other men; they were colliding with women.

"How unfortunate for me," said Burnham, trying to appear *simpatico*.

With a shrug, the direttore replied that perhaps the distinguished *professore* could be accommodated somehow.

For instance, if Burnham was willing to pay a sum in excess of the going rate, some provisions might be made on his behalf. In the late afternoon, when lap swim was over, the pool was not so busy. Merely by avoiding a few obstacles, a skillful navigator could enjoy a decent workout.

"Obstacles?" Burnham asked, as he cautiously counted out bills.

"Children," said the direttore, signing the application blank. "You may begin your training tomorrow."

Mothers brought the children in—lovely young mothers wearing stylish clothes from shops on Via Condotti. Wives of doctors, of lawyers and industrialists, they moved with the offhand pride of the well connected. The ones who had sons in tow marched into the men's locker room just as Burnham, on his first official visit, was taking off his shirt. He might have been embarrassed, but the woman ignored him. They had a job to do. With an amazing combination of tenderness and speed, they stripped their kids and got them into bathing suits. None of the boys was older than seven or eight, but they had learned to be tolerant of unbridled maternalism. Bored as little emperors, they let themselves be kissed, petted, and coddled as the subtle adjustments went on.

When the room was empty again, Burnham changed into his own suit. Cut on a Continental bias, it hid his privates but not much else. Reluctantly, he stood in front of a mirror to take stock of his condition. He saw before him a man in his early forties whose muscles were starting to go slack. It seemed to him that he had too much hair on his chest and not enough at his temples. His full reddish beard looked foolish without its ordinary accompaniment of a tweed coat and a turtleneck sweater. He did not find himself ugly, but beauty was a distant dream.

After a bit of primping, he headed for the pool. It was outdoors, under a fluttery canopy that served as a windbreak. The children were not scattered all around it, as he feared they might be; instead, they were gathered at the shallow end, taking lessons from an instructor, while their mothers observed and commented from a gallery of folding chairs. Slipping into the water, Burnham paddled to a roped-off section where three adults were splashing around. One of them, an old man, was arthritic; the other two, women, shared the professor's trouble with weight.

Burnham swam slow laps across the pool. His shoulders ached, and his joints kept cracking. To divert himself, he thought about food. A vision of shellfish antipasto came into his mind, followed by a plate of veal piccata he'd eaten recently at a restaurant by the Pantheon. He thought next of duck livers on toast, and that made him remember chicken gizzards, rabbit hearts, and a merchant in Arezzo who used to wrap them in newspaper and stuff them into his shopping bag whenever he went to market. Had it really been ten years ago? Back then, he and his wife had lived in a farmhouse, out in the Tuscan countryside. She was pregnant, grandly on display, and this merchant— apron, blue beret—was convinced that innards had a mystical potency which would keep her strong until her term was up. Burnham sautéed them, he disguised them with onions and tomatoes, but she wouldn't touch them, anyway. "I can still taste the blood," she'd say, hitching the waistband of her skirt up over her belly.

At a hospital in Florence, she gave birth to twins. In the ripeness of his emotion, Burnham became converted to the cardinal virtues. From now on, he would be honest, loyal, true. Lighting a ropy black cigar, he sat on the hospital steps and watched the flowing Arno. Water, water. He took what amounted to a vow of simplicity, promising never to ask anything more of life, but in a few years his marriage was over and there he was in a Cleveland hotel, begging an assistant professor of Arabic, a stunning woman, to go to bed with him. As for the twins, Burnham got them every other weekend and for a month in the summer. He had difficulty being around them at first, because they reminded him of his failures as a husband and father, but gradually he came to love them as individuals in their own right whose existence was linked to his as much by accident as by intent.

Switching to a backstroke, he felt the fine beginnings of exhaustion. Traffic noise or not, he would sleep well that night. Even the bellowing TV of the half-deaf couple in the flat above him wouldn't keep him awake. He had tried once to talk to them about the racket, but he insulted the old lady without meaning to, and she got a wooden spoon from her kitchen and almost attacked him with it. What did a foreigner know about proper volume control? Burnham had been angry then, but now, as he drifted placidly along, the incident seemed funny, and he recalled its bizarre highlights until a scream broke his revery.

A blond woman in a scarlet blouse was doing the screaming. She pointed frantically at a vortex in the pool. Out of the froth and bubbles, two skinny arms materialized, flailing like semaphores. Burnham was only yards away, so he swam over and extracted a bug-eyed boy whose panic had given him tremendous power. The kid wriggled and writhed and kept escaping. Twice more he went under before Burnham managed to grab him by the trunks and pull him to a ladder, where the instructor, kneeling, lifted him to safety. His mother dashed to him, tossed a towel over his quaking body, and clutched him to her bosom, crying "Giorgio! Giorgio!" with such passion that the rescue seemed nothing more than an obligatory overture to her operatic grief.

Italians like to worship the heroic, to build cathedrals and monumental statues of the gods, so Burnham became a minor celebrity around the club. The arthritic gentleman, Benito Alfredi, took a particular interest in him. They were often in the locker room together, showering after the boys left, and Alfredi, who was voluble, found it natural to expound on his many concerns. He was mildly crippled in one leg and both hands, but he gave no sign of having noticed and bragged that he was an expert swimmer. This was hard for Burnham to credit, since Alfredi raised such a ruckus with his wild strokes that the chubby women were always complaining. Alfredi himself gave another reason.

"You know why they hate me?" he confided to Burnham in the shower one day. "Because I won't take either of them out. Yes, my friend, I have denied them their deepest craving."

Dressed, the old man resembled a shark off the Via Veneto. He wore a linen blazer and a plum-colored ascot. His trousers came in cream or lime. At least once a week he would ask his new acquaintance to join him for an after-swim espresso, and Burnham, still lonely, would go with him to a café. When Alfredi heard about his research on madonnas, he insisted that they drive immediately to the neighborhood where he'd been born, in Trastevere, to see the finest madonna on earth. They went in his Alfa. The madonna was plaster, set into a niche in the façade of a storefront that housed a pet shop.

For all his goodwill, Alfredi was something of a gossip. He could be nosy and sometimes asked too many questions. Without being invited, he had assumed the role of counselor to Burnham, and he was attentive, in his old-fashioned way, to what he referred to as "romantic affairs." He carried on about Burnham's lack of a companion—which, in a city renowned for the glory of its female population, he deemed a sacrilege.

"Really, Tomasso," he said one evening. "You must take matters in hand. Look at yourself. You're a scholar, a person of eminence, a representative of America, and still you wander around in blue jeans, like a *ragazzo*. You're not nineteen anymore, understand?"

"In the States, we all wear jeans," said Burnham, who enjoyed Alfredi's intensity. Helplessly, he dropped another sugar cube into his cup. "It's no big deal."

"Maybe not to you. But what a Roman girl expects from a mature fellow is a sense of style. As a favor to me, won't you get your hair trimmed? All those hours in libraries, breathing dust—it's no surprise your skin is gray. Me, I keep a year-round tan. At my place on the coast, I stay in the sun for hours, winter and summer. I'll take you there for a weekend when the weather's warmer. In the salt water, I swim even better. I swear, I'm a regular dolphin."

"But I came here to work. Not to play."

"So you spend all your time in Rome writing a book," said Alfredi, unimpressed. "The book gets published, and then what happens? It goes into a library with other books, millions of them, and very slowly it turns to dust. Now, just because I say that, don't go mistaking me for a Neapolitan. I'm not against education. I can even quote you from Montale! 'An underwater brightness flows between us on the belvedere . . .' "

"That's very nice."

"Of course it's nice. It's poetry. But listen to me, Tomasso. What I'm telling you is that you need more balance. You should give yourself a break and go out for a night on the town. A woman would bring out your artistic side. Otherwise, you'll turn into a soldier. A soldier, or a priest."

"I don't want to be a priest," Burnham said.

"And you don't want to be a soldier. This is what I'm saying to you."

Outside the café, people were moving through the streets, buying groceries or stopping for a paper. As Burnham watched their graceful passage, he wondered if Romans took a special comfort from being surrounded by antiquities. After a nation exercised its imperial urge, did it arrive at the equivalent of peaceful, post-athletic relaxation?

"I admire your energy, Benito," he told Alfredi. "When I get a pain somewhere, it slows me down. How do you cope with yours?"

"An intriguing question." Alfredi closed his eyes and meditated before answering. "Here's what I think. The body you see at this table is not the one I live in. I have a memory of another body, the one I had when I was young, and I live in that memory somehow. At the club, if I catch a glimpse of myself naked, with everything showing, I'm shocked. It's me, undeniably, but I also feel that it's *not* me. You shouldn't worry too much about your flesh. Look what happened to Narcissus! The elements will support us, don't you agree? After all, I don't want to burn—I want to melt."

"That sounds like philosophy," Burnham said.

Alfredi patted him gently on the cheek. "No, Tomasso. It's swimming."

One afternoon, the dwarf guard, whose name was Violetta, intercepted Burnham at the gate and gave him a scented envelope. "From Giorgio's mother," she said. Burnham opened it in the locker room while Alfredi looked on. The note inside, from a Maria della Grazia, was an invitation to dinner—a belated "thank you" for Burnham's heroism. "Ha!" Alfredi cackled. "I knew you'd get lucky soon. And she was pretty, too. A little heavy in the hips, perhaps, but that's no sin."

"She's married, Benito."

"Oh, Tomasso!" the old man exclaimed. "Are you truly that naïve?"

Burnham had no desire to travel across town to take a meal with a family of strangers. His remaining time in Rome was already stretched thin. But as he sat around his apartment that evening, hemmed in by piles of manila folders, listening to a Bach partita while sounds of *Dallas* in Italian rained down on him from above, he began to change his mind. What harm would it do to accept? So on Friday night, after putting on a tie and inspecting himself closely, he took a cab to another part of the city, where a light breeze was blowing through a row of Lombardy poplars.

It was Giorgio who responded to his knock, stepping

shyly aside. Burnham would not have recognized him. Slender, with long, fluttery eyelashes, he didn't look athletic at all. Instead, he seemed to have been designed for an artistic pursuit, shaped out of the same raw material as courtiers and poets. All he needed to complete the illusion was a lute under his arm. On his yellow V-neck sweater, which complimented his dark, glossy hair, he had a school crest and a motto in Latin. *"Buona sera,"* said Burnham, extending a hand, which Giorgio solemnly gripped. "I haven't seen you at the club for some time now."

"I don't go there anymore, sir."

"What a pity."

"Not for me." Turning on his heel, he guided Burnham into a handsome parlor done in Milano modern. Every piece of furniture had a double character, simultaneously functional and sculptural. Above the slight odor of leather and plastic, Burnham smelled a roast and realized how pleasant it was to be liberated from the monotony of his own cooking.

"Do you like lamb?" Giorgio asked him.

"Very much."

"Good. It's what we're having. Excuse me now; I will get my mother."

But what about his father? Puzzled by the absence of Signore della Grazia, Burnham took an armchair and leafed through a thick fashion magazine. In a few moments, Giorgio entered the room again, bringing along his mother, graciously, as if he were presenting her at a ball. Over her silk dress, Maria della Grazia wore an apron; heat from the oven had given her face a glow. Her features, like Giorgio's, were fine, and she had a welcoming amplitude that was lacking in the emaciated models Burnham had just been studying. "I am so glad to meet you," she said, an eyebrow arched in humorous appraisal. "You look different with your clothes on, no?"

"This is my usual state," said Burnham, who was charmed.

"Well, they say that clothes make the man."

"Do they say that in Italy?"

"Yes, they do say it." She fanned herself. "It's hot, isn't it? Giorgio, why don't you untie me in back and put away my apron. Then you can fix us some drinks. So, Professore," she said, sitting across from him, "what are you working on here in Rome?"

"I don't have a specific project yet," said Burnham, hedging. He gave a brief description of his monograph. "I've been sifting through documents, searching for an aspect of my field that hasn't been explored."

"For madonnas, you should go to Florence. They have lots of them there."

"I've been to Florence. So has everybody else."

"Yes, I see. Everybody is too many." Giorgio was at her elbow, holding a tray. On it were two cocktails; Burnham eyed them suspiciously. "Don't be concerned," Maria della Grazie told him. "He knows what he's doing. Did you make us Campari-and-sodas, Giorgio? Poor boy, he has had to master so many new things since his father passed away."

Burnham expressed his sympathy. He had been so caught up in conjecture about the absent signore that he suffered a pang of loss. A man, probably about his own age—suddenly gone, transformed into vapors.

"You are very kind," Maria della Grazia went on. "It's been almost two years, but we still have not adjusted. My husband protected us. He took care of things. He paid the bills and did the banking. Sometimes he even bought groceries. That's rare, you know."

"I didn't know."

"Yes, very rare. Because he was a busy man, a financial genius. Everywhere in the country he had clients, and he was always on the road. Actually, he was with a client when he had his accident. The two of them were sailing off Ischia when a storm came up. The boat couldn't handle the waves—or perhaps the client was an incompetent sailor. But I will never be certain. That fellow, he has a hundred different stories!"

"He's alive?"

"Oh yes. Very much alive." She glanced accusingly at Giorgio. "Because *he* knew how to swim."

"I don't want to swim, Mama," Giorgio said.

Sighing, Maria della Grazia got to her feet and began pacing. "I think you know something about psychology, Professore?" she asked.

"I had a few courses when I was an undergraduate." Burnham heard the sound of silk against hose; it affected his ability to speak.

"Well, let me confess that I feel like a candidate for analysis. Never before have I been so unsettled. I have an irrational fear about Giorgio—I am afraid that *he* will drown, too. Yes, I know it's crazy. At the pool, somebody was always watching him. But there are other things to consider. In my head, I sometimes hear a voice that says, 'The water is all around you, Maria.' And then I begin to trace the route Giorgio takes when he goes to school. The bus, it's an old one, with old brakes. It goes by a reservoir.

It follows the river for three miles. Then it goes over a bridge, also very old—from another century."

"Mamma," Giorgio said wearily.

"Don't you talk to me like that!" she cried, scolding him. "It won't be long before some silly girl drags you to the beach, and you'll go diving underwater to show off."

"But I'll be careful."

"No, you won't, Giorgio. Because you are just like your father." Abruptly she quit her pacing. "I am sorry, Professore. But you can see what I'm up against."

"An obsession," Burnham offered, enamored of her high color.

"Correct. And no doubt I should go to a doctor. But the solution is really so simple!" To press her point, she perched on the arm of his chair. "Giorgio, he's a stubborn child. He won't let *me* teach him about swimming, of course—I am only his mother! And even at the club he wouldn't cooperate, because the instructor was insensitive. If you order my son to stay in the shallow part, he will go right away to the deep. Isn't it so, Giorgio?"

"Not every time."

"Yes, every time." She mussed his hair, gazing at him fondly. "But he's a good boy, really. All he needs is someone he can trust."

"Trust is essential," Burnham said.

"Oh, very essential," Maria della Grazia agreed. "Everything in life depends on it."

So over glasses of brandy Burnham and Maria hatched a plot—the professor would take on Giorgio as a special pupil. In the morning he regretted it, but he still felt obligated to keep his word. After a dull bit of research at the Vatican Museum, he rode a bus to the boy's school, where a guard more diligent than Violetta put him through a security check in spite of the arrangements Maria had made. Giorgio was released from his last class a few minutes early. Burnham tried to joke with him, as if he were an older brother. He wanted their time together to be casual, but Giorgio wasn't the casual type. As he trudged along in his bright yellow sweater, his head bowed and his hands locked behind his back, he seemed the very picture of intellectual dread, a miniature Cato whose sole duty it was to defend against any possibility of buoyancy, or fun.

Burnham proceeded with caution. He thought his first step should be to demystify water and rob it of its terror. The Tiber was his destination, and by some clever maneuvering he got Giorgio to join him on a stroll over a path that skirted its banks. Pretending to tire, he stopped at a bench and asked the boy to rest with him for a while. There he delivered an impromptu lecture on the bounty of the river, explaining how it supported fish, crustaceans, and a huge colony of insects; and then he moved outward, in discursive ripples, to embrace the seas and oceans, which were so infinitely complex and populous that they were like a planet within a planet. He spoke also of endurance, and of the utter dependence of the human species on a chemical compound known as H_2O.

"I don't care for science, sir," Giorgio said, leaving the bench to kick at a fallen branch.

Burnham smiled at him. "I just wanted to show you how beautiful the river is. Creatures live in it, you see?"

He watched some larks glide through the sky. "So you don't like science, Giorgio. What is your favorite subject?"

"Music."

"Will you come with me to the club later this week?"

"Well," said Giorgio, hesitating, "we could try."

They met again in a few days. Maria della Grazia brought Giorgio in a taxi. Eager for her company, Burnham urged her to stay for the lesson, but she believed she would make her son nervous and went for coffee instead. In the locker room, Burnham was happy to find that most of the children from the instructional group had already gone home. But three unruly boys were still messing around, snapping towels at each other and examining their genitals, and when they saw Giorgio they hooted at him and shouted insults in a slang the professor couldn't quite grasp. He rose into himself, anyhow, fully adult, and cooled the kids with a single glance of disapproval. At that moment, his compassion for Giorgio was vast.

Music was Burnham's metaphor that afternoon. He pulled shivering Giorgio toward the pool, close to the water but not threateningly so, and demonstrated the crawl and the breaststroke. Giorgio appeared interested and imitated the motions, so Burnham stood behind him, guided his arms, and helped him discover his own rhythm. The boy grew rapturous; his eyes were wide. "Yes, I understand!" he cried. He was swimming in air. Involuntarily Burnham started humming. From his chest, deep down, came a waltz, the beautiful "Blue Danube." On hearing the tune, however fractured or discordant, Giorgio speeded up his tempo and stretched his limbs toward the horizon, floating, a reed through which energy blew.

This was an improvement, surely, but should Burnham call it progress? At his next meeting with Giorgio, when the boy was in gear, he drew him tentatively forward, step by step. For a second or two, he imagined that his pupil might slide into the water without complaint, dreamily, surrendering to the inevitable, but at the last instant Giorgio squirmed free. Not wishing to alienate him, Burnham allowed him to go back to his musical practice strokes, which, more and more, looked like a bastard form of *Tai Chi.* Later on, he coaxed Giorgio to sit on the edge of the pool, dunk his legs, and do some kicking, but as soon as a drop of liquid hit the boy's upper body, he ran away.

As a responsible person, Burnham reported his trials to Maria. She was apologetic, abject—she had asked too great a favor! "No, no," Burnham would say, touching her hand to reassure her; and then he would board a bus for his apartment. All the commuting was costing him time and money, and he had flashes of guilt whenever he passed a library. As his academic fantasies began to fade, his appetite increased. In the evenings, lonely again, he ate three- and four-course dinners; often, it was midnight before he was done. On the way home, he would buy a cup of gelato and think idly about the past, and about the promises he'd made to himself, wondering if his involvement with Giorgio was merely an excuse to avoid work which—even in the best of circumstances—he could never have accomplished.

As spring turned into early summer, the air in Rome got rank and hazy, richly perfumed with diesel exhaust.

Seeking better weather, Benito Alfredi told Burnham he was going to the coast. "Why not come along?" he said. "Bring everybody. I have plenty of room!" Burnham accepted gratefully, and Maria agreed to join him, but only after he'd taken an oath never to let Giorgio out of his sight. They all rode to a sleepy little resort town in Alfredi's Alfa. The town had a yacht harbor, a stone jetty, a bandstand, and many outdoor cafés whose multicolored umbrellas, when viewed from above, had the look of flowers unfolding.

Alfredi's *villino* was a compact two-story house with white walls inside and out. He had named it La Martellata, or the Hammer Blow, because his father, whose fortune had paid for it, used to own a famous marble quarry.

"I worked there for a summer once," Alfredi told his guests, clucking his tongue at the memory. "The noise was loud enough to puncture your eardrums. *Bang, bang, bang!* One summer—and then I went back to the university and earned my degree."

"And what did you become?" asked Maria.

"A graduate with a portfolio of stocks. And I have been one ever since."

In Burnham's bedroom, on the second floor, there was a photograph of quarry workers on a wall, among some marine landscapes. The workers were short but solidly built; their hair was matted and curled, and they had cigarettes in their mouths and marble dust covering their bodies. As Burnham got ready for a swim, he was acutely aware of his own softness. On the beach, among bronzed Italians, it seemed more pronounced than usual. But once he was in the water, he forgot about his deficiencies. He

dived joyously into the surf and took blasts of spray in the
face. Riding in on a wave, he saw Giorgio watching him
from shore—the boy did not answer his salute.

"Isn't it cold?" Giorgio asked him.

"No," said Burnham, tempted to flick some water on the
kid. "It's invigorating. Healthy, you know?"

"Something slimy is on your back."

Burnham peeled off a strand of kelp. "Maybe you'll
come wading with me tomorrow, Giorgio."

"Maybe, sir. But I don't think so."

They strolled around the main plaza that evening.
Tourists packed the streets, and on every block children
were dashing around in loose bunches, their ears pressed
to radios. In alleys, they booted soccer balls at makeshift
goals, or played tag, whooping as they chased one another
over the cobbles. Outside a pastry shop there was a
disheveled man with a monkey on a leash. If anybody
dropped a coin into the monkey's paw, he'd fish a prize
from a burlap sack. Handing over lire, Burnham won a
metal pin in the shape of a dragonfly and gave it to Maria.

For the professor the weekend was a restorative blend
of sun, torpor, and daydreams. As he lay on a mat on the
sand, next to Maria, he would doze off and then wake to
incendiary visions. Heat from the earth, from its core, was
seeping into his bones. By his elbow he had a bucket of
water, and he would pour a cup of it over his head before
periodically scanning the beach for Giorgio. He couldn't
tell if the boy was having a good time. But one thing was
obvious—Giorgio was studying the sea, trying to divine
its nature. For long minutes he stared at it, standing still.
He threw stones into it and watched them disappear.
When gulls flew along its surface, he followed their flight

with a finger. Occasionally he wandered off, approached the wet margin of tide, and then quickly darted away, as if he were being pulled at by a different current entirely, which had its locus in his mother's voice.

"Giorgio! What are you doing down there?"

"Playing."

"I have a nice cold drink for you."

"I'm not thirsty, Mama."

By Saturday afternoon, Burnham was thoroughly relaxed. The soreness and knotted muscles that had plagued him of late had vanished, and he felt youthful and strong. When Alfredi proposed a game of double solitaire before dinner, he agreed to participate, although he couldn't remember the rules. Fashionably attired in a gondolier's shirt and white duck trousers, Alfredi laid out the cards, while Giorgio, forsaking his pile of comics, drew closer.

"I used to play games with my father on this very table," the old man said with a chuckle. "Backgammon, chess, *sett' e mezz'*."

"Did you beat him?" Giorgio asked.

"Never. He was ruthless. If I got ahead, he cheated. To him, losing was the same as being stabbed."

As Alfredi put a seven on an eight, Giorgio said, "I want to learn that game."

"Well, watch us, then," the old man said.

So calm was Burnham that he sat through three rounds before noticing that Maria had gone upstairs. The book she'd been reading marked the spot where she'd been reclining on a couch. When she did not return after a fourth game, Burnham gave his cards to Giorgio, who was very excited, and went to look for her. He found her in her room, sitting on a twin bed. The light was dim and her face was half in shadow, but he could see that she was tired and a bit pale. He asked if she was feeling ill.

"No, I'm fine," she said quietly. "It's lovely here."

"But you're not enjoying yourself."

She raised her head to look at him. "Because I am not a normal person anymore."

"Don't be silly," said Burnham. "Of course you're normal." For emphasis he added, "Things will get better for you, Maria."

"Do you give your word?"

"I give my word." He sat by her on the bed, and she smiled at him. It was one of those rare smiles that come from deep inside, revealing a person's soul.

"My husband, he loved the sea," Maria said, running a hand through her hair. "At night, when he wasn't traveling, we would lie together in the dark, and he would talk about buying a villa in a town like this. Even then, I was sure it would never happen. Always he was moving on to the next thing. Sometimes, when we made love, I could feel him slipping away. He was already outside his skin, you understand? I would ask myself, 'Where is he going?' but I didn't speak of it. In certain ways, I hardly knew him— and that frightens me. Everything passes, and it frightens me." She reached up and gave his beard a little tug. "And now I must deal with this."

"I've had a beard forever," Burnham said, in self-defense. "Otherwise, my face is too round."

Maria smiled more broadly. "It isn't that," she said. "In the village where I grew up, there was a man with a beard like yours. Very bushy and red. He had a grindstone mounted on a cart and visited us to sharpen knives and axes. Any time he was near, I would go hide in the cellar. Irrational! Now look at me with you, Professore."

"Tomasso."

"Yes, Tomasso." She leaned against him. "So here we are."

The kitchen of the *villino* was a large room with tile counters and shelves holding copper pots. When Burnham and Maria came downstairs, they found Alfredi cooking dinner. He was chopping mushrooms and putting pork chops in a casserole. After pouring them some wine, he set out a plate of cheese and olives.

"Your son is the champion of solitaire," he announced gaily to Maria. "And he didn't even cheat."

"Where is Giorgio?"

Alfredi missed her note of concern. "Probably he went to town to celebrate!"

"I'll go get him," Burnham said.

It was dusk, and all along the beach stragglers were collecting their bottles of suntan lotion and packing up their picnic hampers. A cork popped on a terrace, and people laughed and made jokes. Somewhere a dog started to yip. Barefooted, Burnham walked on, beginning to worry—Giorgio had never ventured so far from the house on his own. Down by the water he saw two children digging a moat, and he knelt and asked them if they'd seen a boy of Giorgio's general description. After some whispering, they both pointed to the jetty.

In the distance, against a backdrop of sails, Giorgio was poised on the rocks. He wore his trunks, and he was doing his practice strokes in the air, moving his arms in a supremely fluid way. Burnham shouted to him and then took off at a sprint, but he was too late. Plunging forward, Giorgio entered the sea. Convinced that all was lost, Burnham imagined the child's spiraling descent through kelp and plankton to the sea floor, where his bones would rest for centuries, dissolving. Already he was mourning— poor Giorgio, who was mortal no more! But even as his grief mounted and he began to think of cosmic explanations, as well as excuses for Maria, the boy was struggling up from the depths and then using his eccentric technique to swim to shore. Astonished, Burnham watched him climb onto land and pick up a towel. How could it be? In an instant the professor's happiness was restored. Out of breath, he quit running, hung his head, and felt a sharp pain radiate along his spine. A muscle in his lower back was throbbing. The sensation was familiar to him, but it seemed diminished in intensity, a part of himself to which he could no longer attach much importance. Burnham heard the surf, its varied music, and looked toward the jetty, where a small figure was waving. There was Giorgio, saved again.